KATY WAS MY DELIGHTFUL NEIGHBOR for eleven years. Like her books, there was always something new and refreshing—and sometimes startling— going on in her life. For instance, there was the summer morning when she stepped out of her shower wrapped in a towel and decided to dry her hair while sitting on the back steps. After all, the fields behind her house were always deserted, weren't they?

Well, not that morning. That was the morning truck-loads of hayers suddenly arrived, just as a gust of wind swept through the house, slamming shut both front and back self-locking doors. After much pondering and ingenuity, conducted at breakneck speed, Katy regained entrance by breaking a cellar window. I wonder if the key I suggested she secure outside is still dangling from some secluded tree branch.

I'll let Katy get on with it. She has some stories to tell, I guarantee. . .

Fondly,
Freeda Witham
1992

MAD TUESDAYS

Katy Perry

Illustrated by Lisa Lyons

Perry Publishing
Hallowell, Maine

ISBN 0-9626823-3-0

SPECIAL THANKS to Jean-Paul Poulain for help with the translation
on page 114, and to Joe Phelan for the back cover photograph.

CONTENTS

INTRODUCTION

To me, Katy Perry is a reminder of a way of life that our society seems to have forgotten. Her manner shows that we should appreciate what is around us more than what we can surround ourselves with. She has an uncanny ability to find new depths in seemingly ordinary events. And it is this insight that makes her writing such a special tribute to life in Maine.

There are several outstanding features about Katy that make her unique— not the least of which is her ability to cook. Katy will turn a worthless pile of bones and a few shriveled potatoes into enough soup to last for a week. Katy is the type of person who will wash a plastic bag rather than throw it out. Perhaps her ability to conserve is a habit she picked up during the Depression. It is certainly a wonderful throwback in our modern disposable age.

To those who know her, Katy seems as agile as a seven year old. Just last week I went on a walk with her and I feel it fair to warn you that walking can be just as strenuous an exercise as running; I couldn't keep up with her! In fact, if it weren't for her age I'd swear she's the youngest person I know. She's always doing something. Whether it's washing dishes, mowing the lawn, taking a walk in mid-January, or even writing this book, Katy has never fit the stereotypical image of a grandmother— I should know, I'm her grandson.

I am proud of Katy for these reasons and more. I also hope that you will gain a new sense of pride from the many stories she has written— pride in your own family and home town, and pride in the many pleasures of life in Maine.

—Ian Perry, 18

MAD TUESDAYS

It's little I know what's in my heart,
What's in my mind it's little I know,
But there's that in me must up and start,
And it's little I care where my feet go.
　　　　　　—Edna St. Vincent Millay,
　　　　　　　　Collected Lyrics

VERY WOMAN WORTH her salt deserves at least one day a week to herself. It's no accident the day I take off is usually a Tuesday (already I'm worth my salt, with the Monday wash out of the way). My neighbors know my habits well enough by now to just refrain from answering an early morning call if they would rather have nothing to do with me on that particular Tuesday. For those souls brave or unwary enough to answer the phone, my call often goes something like this: "What *you* got planned for this wonderful day?" (All days off have to be wonderful!).

It may be that the party on the other end of the line does a double take and thinks, "Wonder what the old gal has up her sleeve this time?" The answer is apt to be quite varied, depending on what wheels have been whirling in my head while doing breakfast dishes and making beds. Many factors enter into the final decision—the time of year, kind of weather, shopping to be done—but the trick is turned by mood and the curiosity of the people involved. When we gals have put our heads together and mapped out some impromptu plans, that's it.

Before I go further, I have to say that to follow my prescribed course of action you should be unmarried or have a husband like mine. I would leave him a note about my plans and expected time of return, and he'd have dinner either started or prepared, depending on the length of my excursion. Doubtless he realized that I am more than a little mad, and was either unwilling to cross me or willing to pamper me. If you follow me to this point, then away we go.

The Tuesday jaunt need not be well planned or lengthy. My dear friend and neighbor "Mike" and I have done such diverse things as visit second hand shops (where we both often lose our heads), call on a mutual friend, look up a Swedish sauna, or drive to a remote village with nothing in mind but to look at the points of interest. Some of the most successful Mad Tuesdays have been those for which we had no plans at all, Tuesdays in which we simply gave the car its head and enjoyed the places we discovered.

Almost always, we do find an interesting place or person. This is because we both love to talk to people and, as you know, people nearly always like to talk about themselves! Because we are both naturally curious, we ask questions and that does wonders in drawing people out.

With a weekly vacation from the kitchen and related chores, all the jobs of the rest of the week seem smaller and less important. I recommend it as a way of life. Frankly, I don't suppose it's possible for all women to pursue the flight of abandon I recommend, but I wish you all could. This kind of life was not always possible for me either. When my family was still toddling, I stayed close to the rigging and didn't' mind it a bit. Now with all away, I find lots of empty hours. This is one method I have devised to keep me out of a rut, and stay at least halfway contented as a person.

Doing something completely unscheduled about once every seven days does not bring great returns, unless you consider inspiration and the fresh breath of surprise great returns. I happen to. One of the nicest things about coming home from a Mad Tuesday, is the feeling of utter contentment with my niche in the world. We have to be convinced often, I suspect, that our blessings are tremendous and truly our cup runneth over. Perhaps my very wise husband knew this, and gave me free rein. I tell you, there are hardly any more available just like him.

A MINIATURE CORACLE COMES TO MAINE

Custom is the principal magistrate of man's life.
—Francis Bacon,
Essays of Custom

HEN I FIRST HEARD the word *coracle* I went scurrying to the Funk and Wagnalls to find out what the word meant. Since then, I have not only learned the meaning of the word, I have corresponded with the last known builder of the coracle—and I actually own an original—miniature though it is. But let's take it from the top.

In an article in an international newspaper I learned that the early boats called coracles would soon no longer be made in England. The last man who knew how to build such boats was unable to meet even the small remaining demand for this primitive water craft. The name of the gentleman was mentioned in the article. Being curious, I decided that day that I wanted at least a written word with the gent while he still worked his interesting trade.

The following day an airmail letter was on its way to 8 Severn Side, Ironbridge, England, addressed to Harry Peters. Sooner than I could hope, Harry sent me a reply.

His letter said in part, "I am pleased to learn that news of this ancient craft has reached the States." This, it seems, was not too remarkable because his fame has spread to other foreign lands. In answer to my question, he told me he would be pleased to make me a miniature of the coracle, and it would cost me 15 L 10.

As to the history of the boat, Harry had this to say: "The coracle is a small, rounded boat of hide or oilcloth on a wicker frame. Many claim this odd-shaped vessel is the earliest known form of water travel in the British Isles. There is some thought that this primitive bark has even sailed as far as Iceland. Its fame, however, centers nearer home base. About 60 years ago coracles were very common in the Ironbridge part of Suffolk County. Poachers could easily carry this lightweight craft up the Severn river, net a bountiful catch of fish, and after dusk drift silently back to their homes. They found the coracle as useful for this law breaking as their forefathers had found it to fish legally!"

When I had sent off my return letter to Harry Peters time passed, and no answer was forthcoming. I decided that perhaps without money in hand, wise Harry would have nothing to do with me. I had, however, truly underestimated the man. I had probably underestimated the time needed for surface mail as well.

Nearly six months passed before I received an interesting package—rather badly beat up. It was wrapped in several layers of brown paper and secured with black tape, similar to the kind electricians use. Inside was a box, again wrapped, labeled, and wound around and around with the same black tape. Making my way through this, I finally unearthed a miniature coracle, complete with paddle,— everything securely tied within the box to keep it stationary.

As far as I know, the only miniature coracle in the state of Maine, perhaps in New England, is now proudly resting on my coffee table. What can one do with it, you ask? In truth, this interesting boat performs no useful function—except to generate questions by those who have never before seen the like.

Rather egg shaped, with a three-inch center board, our coracle measures 8 inches wide by 10 inches long, by 3 inches deep. A wide strap of rawhide laces through holes in the center board. Positioned across the boatman's chest, this strap, on a full sized coracle, would permit the lightweight boat to be balanced effortlessly on his back. Frame ribbing in the miniature is beautifully varnished and forms a pleasing pattern. Tarred cloth is stretched over the frame to provide a good strong body. The entire structure looks simple enough, and elegant in its simplicity. I feel fortunate to have this treasure, suspecting that nearly as much time and effort went into the miniature as would be needed for a full-size boat.

THE WEDDING GUEST

I wish you all the joy that you can wish.
—Shakespeare
Merchant of Venice,
Act III, Scene 2

 HE SPRING OF 1941 was bright and promising as we graduated from Farmington Normal School in the Franklin County Shiretown. Politically, however, the clouds of war already hung over the graduates and descended in earnest later in the year to interrupt the plans of many of my classmates. But for my roommate, Marilyn Chillis, and her fiance, Dick Bell, the only plans were wedding plans, and they went forward.

Marilyn's family were early settlers in the charming village of Somesville, lapped by the tides of Somes Sound, a beautiful waterway that nearly bisects Mount Desert Island, just off the Maine coast. It was not surprising, then, that Marilyn and her parents wanted the wedding to take place in the century-old clapboard church just steps from their comfortable home. It would be the first wedding in the building in decades.

I was flattered when Marilyn asked me to be her Maid of Honor and to sing before the ceremony. I worked at nearby

Asticou Inn in Northeast Harbor that summer, and spent many hours practicing wedding music and being fitted for a gown.

The August day was beautiful and the church over-flowed as the bridal party arrived. I took my place at the front of the church with the organist and after I had "wowed" the assemblage with my rendition of "Oh, Promise Me," I walked to the back of the church to find the wedding party agog with chatter and amazement. Helen Hayes, the actress, and her young daughter and son were in the audience!

I gulped more than a few times. I had sung before such a famous personage! Thank heavens I hadn't known before the song.

Even though Helen Hayes did nothing to call attention to herself after the ceremony, people were anxious to speak to her and take her picture. She was most gracious, as you know she would be, and left rather quickly. It was not her intent, surely, to intrude on a day that belonged to the bride. No doubt about it, though, her presence enhanced the excitement of the day.

That year Miss Hayes had taken a small cottage at Somesville and undoubtedly had heard much about the upcoming wedding. A church ceremony does not require an invitation and I suspect, although I do not know this for a fact, she simply wanted her children to experience what it would be like to live in a small community and become part of the life of that community. I learned a good lesson that day in poise, for Helen Hayes has that quality to perfection.

MARY GOSLINE PARKER:

STILL ON THE GO

*It is not the brains that matter most, but that
which guides them—the character, the heart,
generous qualities, progressive ideas.*
  —Fyodor Dostoyevski,
  The Insulted and the Injured

MARY GOSLINE PARKER, at 94, looked back over a life that would be perfect for a Neil Simon play. Brought up as a farm girl in Gardiner, Mary went on to become a secretary to prominent people in the world of high fashion and marketing. Because of her knowledge of the French, she became a foreign correspondent on the subject of a major restoration project in Paris.

Mary was, as well, campaign manager for both a Maine congressman and a Maine governor, an associate editor of *Travel Magazine*, a feature writer for *Mademoiselle Magazine* and a publicity writer for American Airlines.

Mary's early childhood was spent in both Worcester, Massachusetts, her birthplace, and a home in New Brunswick, Canada. At the suggestion of relatives, the family moved to Gardiner, Maine. Her father was a farmer and a salesman for *The Maine Farmer*, a popular publication in the early 1900s.

"My father was sire of all the Goslines that now live in the Gardiner area," Mary told me. "There are many of us!"

After graduating from Gardiner High School in 1910, Mary went to Mount Holyoke College, where she studied languages, a choice that served her well in later years.

"I taught school in Tarrytown, New York for a time," she remembers. "After taking a civil service exam I was hired as a translator preparing data for the Versailles peace conference. When that was completed, I was hired to prepare a vegetational survey of South America and I worked in the basement of the Department of Agriculture building in Washington with another young woman. It was a horrid boondoggle, but we completed the survey and were even given credit for the work by the American Geographical Society."

The years 1924-25 were exciting ones for Mary. She spent that time in Paris, working with Anne Morgan of the financially prominent Morgan family of New York.

"Anne Morgan had spent a great deal of time, money and effort during and after World War I working with French people whose lives had been upset or interrupted by the war. Because I spoke French," Mary continued, "I became her typist. It was fascinating work and I met many wonderful people including Premier Henri Tardieu, with whom Miss Morgan worked."

One such activity was the restoration of a pavilion in the Chateau Blerancourt. "The Germans had taken the bells from the pavilion and melted them down, I suppose," said Mary. "They were recast and rededicated in a charming ceremony. Each bell was "dressed" in blue satin and white lace, if you can imagine such a thing. After the blessing they were disrobed and rung. These bells were inside the church and you cannot believe the tremendous clamor they made. It was truly quite wonderful!"

Upon returning to Maine, Mary was asked to handle the

political campaign of John Nelson of Augusta. He was running for the U.S. Congress. John was victorious and Mary followed him to Washington expecting to stay his term, but Tudor Gardiner called her home to help him with his gubernatorial campaign. She came back and he won.

Mary had always wanted to write. Believing in her own ability, she returned to New York and made the rounds of many of the popular publications of the day. Winsome ways and native ability paid off. She became associate editor of *Travel Magazine* and a few years later *Mademoiselle*, where she felt "There had to be a place for me to tell young ladies about something other than the clothes and beaus their minds were choked with."

The column she initiated with *Travel Magazine* was called "Look Where You're Going"— not bad wisdom at any time and a philosophy she still uses.

When I spoke with her recently, Mary was retired and living the life of a country lady. She enjoyed every moment of the day as she surveyed the vista of rolling fields and small ponds from the comfort of her Gardiner parlor. She returned to Maine in 1955.

In her 95th year Mary Gosline Parker was still making plans. The travel bug that bit her years ago was still alive, and Mary was off to England. Her trip included a visit to the English Lake District where her late husband's family still owned a castle.

Of her 95th birthday, Mary announced, "I'm giving myself a party, and you need not look for lots of food or entertainment, just good conversation."

TWO BURIALS AT PREBLE CEMETERY

*Father declared he was going to buy a new plot in the cemetery,
a plot all for himself. "And I'll buy one on the corner,"
he added triumphantly, "where I can get out!"*
—Clarence Day,
Life with Father

 ENRY WATERS WAS A PRINCE of a
fellow. In fact, his many friends re-
ferred to him affectionately as Prince.
Prince, his wife and son were the seventh generation to spend summers at
their small home along Route 218 in
the Kings Mills section of Whitefield.
Henry was a history buff who spent hours collecting
letters, family diaries and personal journals. Among his sources
was a handwritten book that detailed a great deal of history of
the people in that rural settlement. The Prebles, the Hapgoods,
Kennedys, Waters, Turners—each had a section in the book
detailing life during the first years of the century. Although
the book belonged to the Preble family, it was Henry Waters
who copied out by hand the following account of a 1910
burial in the small family plot where my very dear friend,
Margaret Brisbine Preble is also interred.

The day after Margaret's 1970 funeral I attempted to
describe the scene in a manner similar to the way Eglantine
Preble had recounted the burial of her father. Surely I have

fallen far from the mark. Let me defend myself with the comment that a November funeral, even with the colorful leaves of autumn, is a somber ceremony compared to an early summer ceremony where wild flowers and bouquets from friendly gardens dominate.

● ● ●

Sunday, November 22, 1970
The interment of the ashes of Margaret Brisbine Preble

The seventh anniversary of President John Kennedy's assassination was marked in Whitefield, Maine by the interment of a beautiful woman, Margaret Brisbine Preble. Margaret's two devoted stepsons had brought her ashes to Whitefield following a funeral ceremony at the Huguenot Presbyterian Church in Pelham Manor, New York on Friday, November 20.

The Sunday morning dawned clear after Saturday's intermittent rain. A mild wind warmed rather than pierced those who gathered for the ceremony.

Joe and Neota Grady carried Emma Chase, and were the first to arrive. Shortly after, Bernie and Katy Perry drew up at the drive to the Preble house and joined the others. The Reverend Mr. Biggs from the North Whitefield Church walked toward them from the house, saying he would await the others nearer the plot. Cars parked along the road that bordered the field with the burying yard beyond. Roger and Dick Preble drove up from the house, Dick carrying a small package. Bob and Ray Hutchinson with two of their children, Gail and John, arrived with Margaret's two sisters, Catherine Cook and Evelyn White (Evelyn had passed the night with the Hutchinsons). With them was a friend from Rockland, Richard Stevens.

The next car carried the Reverend Leonard LeClair, chaplain at the V.A. hospital at Togus, with one of Margaret's friends, Mrs. Henry Pollock ("Mike"). Rollie and Hoddy (Roland and Horace) Kennedy joined the group. Having left their tractor at the neighbors', they would reclaim it at the conclusion of the ceremony and continue their farm chores.

A small Volkswagon arrived next, with Dorothy Kensell Palmer and her son, Rundlette. These two were perhaps the nearest kin to Roger and Dick Preble. Evelyn and Joseph Goodavage and their two children, Danny and Maria came along on foot. The Goodavages are living in the lovely ancestral Preble home.

Introductions took place as the group made its way toward the leaf-strewn cemetery plot. The iron chain which customarily kept the plot separate from the outside world had been lowered.

Roger and Dick stepped forward and together lifted the small package which had been placed at the edge of the grave. Dick slipped off the chamois cover, revealing a bronze box. The two men lowered the box into the ground. Dick stepped back and Roger, with careful exactitude, settled it into the place he felt proper. Both the Reverend Biggs, from the local Union Church, and Father LeClair said prayers at graveside. Margaret, who had painted portraits of both men, would have been pleased with their attendance.

As the group began to disperse, Evelyn Goodavage invited all to come to the house for a cup. Roger Preble took up the shovel from the spot where Joe Goodavage had thoughtfully left it the day before when he dug the grave, and began to cover the plot. Joe shepherded the group toward the gate to the house. Only the leaden autumn sky and the slightly waving trees bore witness as Roger painstakingly covered his stepmother's remains and smoothed the ground.

Soon more leaves will fall and make this new grave look as familiar and comfortable as those that have been crowned by decades of autumn leaves.

Margaret Brisbine Preble might have chosen to be buried in South Dakota, where she was born, or in Texas near her mother and father. She might well have chosen to be placed beside her first husband Enzo Baccanto and her small daughter in a cemetery in New York City. Instead she chose to rest in this small, rural Maine family burying plot near her second husband, Theodore Preble, and his kin.

Circumstances ruled otherwise. Though the marker at the site states that Margaret and Ted are buried there, Ted's ashes are lost. In 1967, two days before his burial ceremony was to have been held, vandals had broken into the Preble house. Along with all Margaret's legal papers, checkbooks and address books, her clothing and other personal belongings, they took the brass urn containing Ted's ashes. It has never been located.

● ● ●

Excerpts from a letter written by Eglantine Preble to her mother after the burial of her father, Abraham Preble, 1910. The burial was in the Preble burying ground, Whitefield, Maine.

This A.M. the dear folks finished the work at the yard. They asked me not to go out until all was done, so I did not go out until it was time for the services to begin. Two boys, Eddie Blair and Warren Cunningham, made the grave (and filled it up at last, both hard pieces of work). Then they covered every bit of the earth with green branches, so that no part in or out of the grave was in sight.

Along the slope of the mound they put flowers and flower pieces made largely of wild flowers. Helen made one of pansies and clematis blossoms, Aunt Esther Hopkins, one of sweet peas and ferns, and Louise and Lena, one of pearly everlasting with the word "Love" in purple pansies across it. One of the children said it was everlasting love. Eva and Freda got water lilies and ferns and one of ferns, clematis and sweet peas for the coffin lid. Poor Ann came up this morning and put a little bunch of flowers on the coffin at the house and said to Ellery, "I put that there because he was good to me and I love him."

Gene Preble came over from Jefferson. The G.A.R. came with a flag and stood in a body at the head (Wm. Dancer and Oscar Boynton were all I knew). Annie Walker, Thirza Percy and Weston sang "Some Happy Day," then "Jesus, Lover of My Soul," then "Face to Face." George King is a good boy with a pulpit manner, but I like him. He read about half the service in the ritual and a rather short address, which was good. He spoke mostly of Father's Christian life and how much young people liked him and things people had told him. Then Forest asked everyone to put a sprig of green in the grave (as the G.A.R. do) and to come in an informal way to the coffin. Most of them did. E. and Katie Hatch [cousins] did not come over and then came to speak to me.

After the mound was shaped the girls covered it entirely with green, and then placed the flowers about very prettily and naturally, what was not in dishes. The whole thing and the yard looked beautiful.

The monument they draped in a long made piece of

evergreen boughs. All the people about worked on the yard. The only gap in the trees that surround it now is the gate. Everybody said, "How beautiful and sweet it is here!"

We shall keep everything fresh as long as possible. I took off the button and badge the last thing, and put some of Eva's pond lilies and Amy's bunch of oleander and Ann's poor little nosegay inside the coffin. Forest Ware said the embalming was perfect and there was no change or disturbance.

A CHAT ON HATS

You see, dear, it is not true that Woman
was made from Man's rib. She really
was made from his funny bone.
—James Barrie,
What Every Woman Knows

HEN MY KIDS were young, Captain Kangaroo was the hottest thing on the tube. They spent mornings—and not too many hours of those mornings—watching the Captain and Mr. Green Jeans subtly teaching aspects of life to growing youngsters. A neighboring doctor enjoyed the programs with his kids as much as the kids did.

One of the ways the Captain introduced youngsters to professions was through the hats people wore. A fireman's hat, a fisherman's, policeman's, big game hunter's, doctor's, nurse's, almost every kind of headgear provided a new exposure for the viewer. I especially liked that segment when it flashed on the screen and stopped whatever I was doing in our country kitchen to join the boys. You see, I have a great affection for hats. I am pleased there seems to be a new interest in them.

My interest undoubtedly started with my mother. In the '20s, ladies' hats were large, luxurious and festive even in a remote, wooded town such as Millinocket. Mother talked often of Mrs. Ryan, who made her living sewing chapeau for local ladies. She was a beautiful Irish woman who sewed veils and netting to basic straw hats in a special section of Rush's Ladies Store. At Easter time the window of this store challenged many a Fifth Avenue boutique in finery. Mrs. Ryan set the tempo for elegance in that town.

Even with limited space in my small house, I can't bear to separate myself from some hats that date back to 1945! There is one I bought in Bangor with my first pay check. Of multi-colored wool with a jaunty brim and tall, pinched-in crown, it would remind you of something Gloria Swanson might have worn. It has not been worn for decades— but is part of my war years memorabilia and as such will stay in my closet.

Then there is a brown felt number that I bought at Augusta's Community Exchange back in the early '60s. It is shaped like a British Tommy's helmet and boasts a mustard colored stripe running from back to front. It is elegant. The body of it was made in Austria and carries a label stating it was designed by Hattie Carnegie. It radiates haute couture and I have worn it seldom, but I can't part with it.

When mother was married for the second time, I helped select a graceful black straw to complement her tailored suit. It fit her regally and she looked lovely. I am not sure if it's for sentiment or because it's such a lovely feminine piece that I cling to it, but it also rests in a tissue-wrapped box on my closet shelf.

Those of you who know me may recall seeing the soft two-tone (white and beige) llama hat I wear in colder months. This cover was only one of several I brought back from a brief visit to Peru. It is wondrously warm, and quite a smashing hat,

I think. The fact that it is real fur causes me some concern, but the deed was done when I saw it first, so I didn't hesitate too long in making the purchase. I hope to wear it for many more years, alternating it with a dark brown and a white felt that came from the same country.

Over the years I have knit, crocheted and sewed many hats, some that turned out dreadfully, and others that, although not works of art, did a good job of keeping the head warm.

So there's much to be said for hats, at least in my house. I truly believe that there is great merit in wearing a head cover during the colder days. This fact was firmly established on a camping trip to Greece.

Chris, the tour leader, insisted we cover our heads during the cold nights as we tented along country streams. One evening my tent-mate, an older Canadian woman, was visibly shivering as Chris checked each tent before she turned in.

"Dorothy!" she exploded, "You're shivering. I told you to cover your head." With that Chris rushed out of the tent and quickly returned carrying a wool scarf. This she hastily wrapped around Dorothy's exposed head. She tucked a blanket around her shoulders and lower body, remarking as she left, "Now cuddle down and get to sleep!" Both Dorothy and I responded to this demand.

For fashion, ceremony, identification, or a personal statement, hats and caps are here to stay. They are the most compelling part of a lady's wardrobe, I think— as the poets might say, a "crowning glory."

THE BLESSING OF HOME BAKED BREAD

Food is a weapon.
—Maxim Litvinov to Walter Lyman
Brown of the Hoover Mission,
Riga, 1921

 "THE ONLY WAY to make good bread is to keep making it." I can almost see Dot Waugh's eyes sparkle as she gave me my first lesson in making bread. That was 1946. 45 years later I'm still making bread the same way, and I still use the same tattered, dough-smeared card I wrote Dot's recipe on. She was right—keep on making it week after week, and you too can bake a tolerable loaf of the staff of life.

At Christmas time I add candied fruit to the same basic recipe and, voila—fruit bread that makes elegant toast for Christmas morning. By flattening out a good-sized blob of dough, brushing butter on it, adding brown sugar and chopped nuts, then rolling and twisting it into a circle, it becomes a coffee ring. When I feel particularly thin—and somewhat festive, I cover the cooled twist with a thin icing.

Dot Waugh's same bread recipe makes elegant rolls. One year I made 12 dozen finger rolls for a bridal shower. When I gave the recipe on a radio show I had a dozen requests for it.

It has always been my contention that when you take time to bake, you might as well get way into the thing and make twice as much as you need and freeze the rest. I've doubled, tripled and, on one very ambitious occasion, quadrupled a batch. A word to the wise, that was too much—way too much.

People reading this may have learned other cooking techniques from Mrs. Maurice (Dot) Waugh. Dot taught home economics in Millinocket in the '20s and again in the late '40s. Her ability as a cook was surpassed only by her ability as a seamstress.

Reluctantly I admit I've had some singular failures in baking bread, but I like to think it's only because I'd had my hands out of the dough dish too long, and the failure was in no way a reflection on my culinary ability.

When colder weather comes on and you feel an urge to be part of the growing trend to do things "from scratch," you might like to try what has always been at our house, Dot Waugh's bread.

ROLLS AND BREAD
Dot Waugh, 1946

1 cup milk	2 tablespoons sugar (+)
2 cups water (hot)	2 yeast cakes
1 teaspoon salt (+)	2 eggs (optional)
4 tablespoons butter	6 cups flour

Scald milk. Add salt. Add 1 1/2 cups hot water. Let

cool. Dissolve yeast in 1/2 cup cooled water to which sugar has been added. Add eggs and flour until dough forms. Knead lightly . Put in pan and grease top. Let rise (about 2 hours in a warm room). Knead lightly again. Put in pan, grease top, and let rise (about 1/2 hour). Bake 425°, 15 to 20 minutes. Lower heat to 325°. Finish baking until golden brown!

Any good, basic bread recipe, however, will serve you very well. You would not believe the tremendous therapy kneading bread is. And the nicest thing about bread, you know, is that even if the finished product is inedible, the combination of yeast, flour and milk makes the most heavenly smell in the kitchen!

MAINE OCTOBER
CAN THROW YA'

The inner half of every cloud
is bright and shining;
I therefore turn my clouds about,
And always wear them inside out
To show the lining.
—Ellen Thorneycroft Fowler,
The Wisdom of Folly

I F GOOD OLD CRISTO COLUMBO arrived, not in the Caribbean but on the shores of Maine's coast in autumn, what do you suppose his thoughts would be? If the weather were as nippy as it can be in Maine, he would undoubtedly hustle the crew back aboard and shove off for warmer climes. But wait.

Perhaps the foliage would intrigue him enough to urge the official artist to get out his paints and capture the splendor in a tribute to his patron when they returned to Hispaniola. Perhaps she wouldn't believe the colors that Maine and, for that matter, all of New England boasts at this time of year.

Another stopper for the old sailor might be the massive mounds of granite along the shore. Wouldn't the sculptors back home have a chiselling fest working those rugged chunks of rock!

All this to say nothing of the modern machines he would find. Could he comprehend the fact that his arrival would have been known long before his sails were spotted? Or that there would be a television crew ready to record every move the crew made lowering the sails and readying the craft for landing, or that Queen Issy and King Ferdie would already know he had found a "new" land.

It's easy to believe sighting land was a welcome relief to the sailors after months crossing unknown waters. 57 years ago on Columbus Day I felt something of the same relief when my mother and I finally arrived at Aunt Eva's house in Milo. It happened like this:

My mother worked in Augusta and I lived with her. My brother John was with Mother's sister in Milo. It had been arranged that during the Columbus school vacation Mom and I would plug 50 cents worth of gas in the Model A Ford and drive the 100 miles north to visit. All of us looked forward to the occasion. We were lonesome for each other.

We had an uneventful trip almost to Clinton when small flakes of snow began to hit the windshield. It was cold outside and not much warmer inside the car. Mother said nothing. Neither did I, but I gulped a lot. Mother didn't have a lot of driving experience, and snow was not making her especially happy with her lot. We both reasoned it was a momentary squall. Not true.

As we headed into Newport and turned off toward Dexter and Dover-Foxcroft, the snow thickened, far more than the occasional flake. By Sebec, the road was invisible. Mother opened the window to keep her eye on the side of the road. Now and then a car passed going the other way, slowly, and once or twice almost in the ditch. As is often the case with early snow, the warmer road turned the falling snow into salve. Keeping on the roadway demanded constant attention. A slight twist of the wheel and it was the ditch for us.

Small chatter hardly helped. We were both absorbed

with our voyage, prayerful it would end safely. The final hurdle was a long, winding hill that would bring us down into Milo. I don't know about Mom, but I had closed eyes all down that slippery slide. We made it. Obviously she was fully intent on her work.

Absolutely no comparison between the two journeys, but I think I can sense the relief the Nina, Pinta and Santa Maria's voyagers knew when they sighted land that October, 1492. Mom never received any medals for her driving ability, but as I reflect on that eerie drive so many years ago, I have no qualms about giving her a well-above-average mark for a job well done.

CERTAIN OF HER VOTE

*A lovely lady, garmented
in light from her own beauty.*
　　　　—Percy Bysshe Shelley,
　　　　The Witch of Atlas

 HE PRIVATE half-hour I was privileged to spend with former U.S. Senator Margaret Chase Smith in her charming living room overlooking the Kennebec River will always remain a vivid memory.

Because I was to be in Skowhegan one afternoon, I called Northwood Institute's Margaret Chase Smith Library Center to learn how to contact the lady.

"I'll give you her telephone number. Call her," was the polite gentleman's response.

"Is there a secretary or someone I should contact?" I asked.

"No. She will probably answer herself," he said. She did. Senator Smith indicated she would be pleased to see me and asked that I come to her door through the library center.

At the appointed hour I rang the bell. Slightly stooped, gray-haired Margaret Chase Smith came to greet me. She wore the traditional red rose on her classic blue dress with a double strand of pearls her only adornment. Her warmth made me feel like a VIP rather than a first-time aspiring Maine legislator. As I followed her into the house it occurred to me that I was being welcomed as graciously as Margaret Thatcher or Nancy Reagan would be. I doubt this Maine lady rarely, if ever, has been overawed by personal power or famous people—an important lesson for anyone interested in the political arena.

We began our conversation with my reason for asking to see her. I hoped she would share some hints or impart her own successful philosophy about holding office.

She began by telling me why she was seen as a liberal. "I have always been a registered Republican, but I think it was in the early '40s, when I voted to extend the draft, that people considered my views more liberal than they expected. I had studied the issue very thoroughly," she said, " and I voted as I felt I must. I think history has proved it was the right way."

"It was later in that decade," she continued, "about 1946 or '47 when the Lend-Lease issue was being debated. Maine people were very opposed to it. In fact, a very good friend, an attorney in the state, was insistent I vote against the proposal. He telegraphed me often about his feelings."

"The day after the vote was taken," Senator Smith continued, "the New York Times announced the votes. I got a blasting letter from my friend. He could not believe I voted as I did. I answered his letter with a note saying simply that I had to have the flexibility to vote any issue as I saw it needed to be voted, and that I was sorry he was upset."

There was just a hint of merriment in this statement. "A few weeks later I met him at a dinner party. When he saw me he rushed to me and gushed, 'I expected a thrashing for my letter.' I assured him that all that was past and best we forget

CERTAIN OF HER VOTE ◆ 39

it. He had done what he felt he must do, and so had I.'

"You see," she went on, "in my position I had to be certain of my vote. Whichever way I voted, I had to live with the decision for the rest of my life. It's quite another thing to feel a thing is right today and be able to change your mind tomorrow. I did not have that luxury. Some time later my friend came to me and said he had since seen that in following my conviction I had voted the right way. That, of course, pleased me."

I asked how she felt about United Sates foreign policy in relation to Central America (this was in April, 1988). "I would not want to comment on that at all," she answered. "I have no knowledge on which to base a judgement. In fact, I find the entire Contra situation too complicated to comprehend. It's dangerous to make a judgement simply on what you read in the papers."

I asked about how Northwood Institute had been selected as custodian of her papers.

"Well," she began, "that is something of a long story. It was about the early '70s, I think, that a group of quite influential Maine businessmen—people who were great friends and supporters of mine, asked my plans for memorabilia and other things that were the result of my service in the U.S. government. I told them quite frankly that I was not finished with the work I had to do. I appreciated their interest and when the proper time came, I would be happy to talk with them. I think they had some thought of raising funds for a library."

Senator Smith went on, "Princeton University had approached me asking if they might become a repository of my papers. The University of Maine at Orono made a similar request. I was really quite receptive to this interest."

My administrative assistant, Bill Lewis, said to me one day, 'Senator, you know the Governor of Maine has some sway over the University system. It's conceivable that some future governor may see fit to pack your works away and store them far from public eye. That seems a possibility you might consider before you make a decision.' Mr. Lewis always had my best interests in mind, and I did indeed give the comment careful thought."

A series of events after this conversation with Bill Lewis determined the future of Margaret Chase Smith's accumulation of work.

"I was named a "Distinguished Woman' by Northwood Institute in Midland, Michigan. To receive the award, I traveled to their campus and was most impressed not only with the facility but with its two founders, Dr. Arthur Turner and Dr. Gary Staugger. Some time later I attended a dinner meeting of the Institute in Chicago. Mr. Lewis accompanied me, and I was surprised when a waiter came to our table, tapped Bill on the shoulder and told him Doctors Turner and Stauffer wanted to see him. A bit later I found out Northwood had asked to establish a campus, in my name, in Skowhegan. They would build a library as a meeting place and reference and resource center where my personal effects and papers would be available for the use of future scholars," she explained.

"The press had a real time with the idea when it was announced. 'Margaret Chase Smith has turned her back on her native state—all that sort of thing. I responded by asking when it had become possible to uproot land and transfer it to another state. You see, they did not comprehend at all what was really going to take place. Well, finally the turmoil ceased and we now have what I believe to be a beautiful facility here attached to the home I will be in as long as I live. After my demise the home will be turned into a museum and continue to benefit students . You know, the library itself, beyond my papers and memorabilia, is very impressive," she said.

We turned then to the original reason I had been bold enough to ask for her time, some thoughts I could use in waging a political campaign.

"Well," said Senator Smith, "things are quite different today than when I ran for office. I did not do fund-raising as it's done today. During election day we carried voters who were without transportation to the polls. Many of my friends used their cars, and if they needed gasoline, why I paid for it out of my pocket. I have always felt it is wise not to be too firmly attached to any single-issue organization. I still do. Try to keep your campaign simple and do not ally yourself with any group. You need to be able to do your own research, seek the dictates of your constituency and make up your own mind. In fact, I often voted in a manner that upset the people I was elected to represent, but—knowing all the background of each bill and having close access to committee reports and hearings— I felt I was in a better position to make decisions even if they were seen as wrong by the people back home. It was not an easy balance, I can tell you, but that's the way I operated."

She continued, "Beyond that, it was important that I not divulge my thinking until it was time to vote. Some of the media did weekly polls. When they asked me, I would tell them if I knew how I was going to vote today, there would be no further need to attend hearings and committee meetings in the weeks to follow. It upset many of them, you can be sure, but that is the way I operated then, and I would still operate that way if I were in the Senate today."

In typical Smith fashion, the lady summarized her previous statement. "To vote my conscience, to talk little or not at all about my thoughts, to study the issues at hand and carefully weigh what I learned against comments from my constituency, all took place before a decision was made to vote 'yes' or 'no'. Once made, I stuck to it. Oh, if I saw at some future date that I had voted unwisely, something I rarely felt, I was not intimidated. Perhaps that assurance in your own judgement comes from doing the job for so many years. I must say the assistance of a capable businessman is invaluable. I was privileged to have the help of Bill Lewis and greatly valued his counsel. The ability to discuss my votes with such a learned, understanding person was truly helpful."

Our conversation had gone on for some time, I realized as I looked at the beautiful French porcelain clock tucked among the books in the soft green bookcase. I feared I had already tired this alert lady just past her 90th birthday. When I mentioned overstaying my visit, she apologized for overspeaking!

I was more than a little tempted to scan other bookshelves and tables in the room, for each held fascinating objects. Here and there was a single red rose tastefully arranged in a silver or crystal vase. Instead, we both stood looking out the large windows down the neatly groomed lawn to the Kennebec sparkling below, full of rushing April water, and beyond to the bustling skyline of Skowhegan's business streets. We agreed, almost in unison, that the vista was marvelous in its New England beauty.

I picked up my purse. Margaret Chase Smith held my coat and ushered me to the door at the end of an inviting solarium. As we said our good-bys she thanked me for coming with a sincere, "Now do come by again."

I walked back around to the entrance of the library center to take another look at the books, citations, photos, events and cherished mementoes in the life of this unique lady from Maine. As I drove away the thought struck me that I had been in the presence of a person who has known and worked with most of the important heads of state throughout the world for over 30 years. She had chatted with me as if I were a longtime friend.

Time Magazine once named Margaret Chase Smith "Woman of the Year." Maine knows a person of her stature will rarely if ever come our way again. Thank you, Senator Smith, for my introduction into your life.

MAKING SOMETHING
OUT OF NOTHING

The man who lets himself be bored
is even more contemptible than the bore.
—Samuel Butler,
The Fair Haven, 1873

 HEN YOU LIVE along the coast and pick up wood, you call it driftwood. If your home is near an inland lake and you're in the habit of picking up bits of debris along the shore, then you call it by its Indian name, "dri-ki" (pronounced "drī kī"). Either way, what you have acquired can become an interesting conversation piece, a decorative ornament, or the means whereby you slowly work yourself out of garage, attic, and eventually, home.

Unfortunately, there is no known cure, as yet, for the madness known as driftwood fever. What starts out as an innocent single acquisition soon becomes a compelling force that makes every drive one that somehow passes the most likely spot to scan the shore for just one little piece. The only consolation is the fact that there are thousands of others who feel just as moved by a gnarled old tree root as you do. Misery does love another miserable driftwood addict. Though the fever will probably never abate, there is reason to believe that, given the nature of the addict, the focal point of interest may shift to some other strange bit of nature—perhaps rocks or sea shells.

The dri-ki addict (to whose creed I subscribe) would consider it unthinkable to venture forth without a small saw. There is always the possibility of making the find of all finds, and you have to be ready to sever the treasure from the junk.

But be warned—light effects make strange bits of wood even stranger or lovelier. It's amazing how often what looks like a fabulous find in the twilight looks more like kindling in the light at home. In the same way, the junk you just tossed in at the end of the trip may be the best piece you own.

Sturdy shoes are the only other necessity for a wood-hunting trip. It's always the most remote piece, the one way out of reach in the water that has to be salvaged. Let's make those sturdy shoes waterproof, too. So, armed with saw and shoes, here we go.

As any bit of imagination can create a story or a painting, so it will discover mysterious possibilities in a bit of driftwood or dri-ki. You may decide to save a particular piece because if you turn it one way it looks just like a dog. The next one may have the rhythm of a swan with grace and symmetry in every line. Sometimes a large, many-limbed piece is selected for purely utilitarian reasons—it's a darn good place to hang your hat!

People may like collecting these bits of wood because anyone can do it and it's one of the few joys left that's free except for the strain of gathering. If you wish to do your picking on private property, however, be sure to get permission to be on the land long before you start your collecting.

In speaking with a game warden at a remote lake in northern Maine, I asked if many people carried away bits of driftwood. A warm smile spread over his face as he answered in the affirmative.

"Yep! Couple from New York drive in here every summer. They come to one of the nearby sporting camps to fish. She was the one used to wander around and pick up pieces of dri-ki. Her husband sat in the car and worked on a crossword puzzle, muttering to himself all the time she was gone. They did this for a couple of years. Last three or four years they been coming back, he's just as loco as she is. You can hear her over in the cove yelling 'Oh, I've found just the right piece for a lamp.' Then you can hear him from the other direction—'I've found the base for your lamp over here!' It's getting so now, they leave here trying to decide if they can afford to rent a U-haul back to New York, or if they can stow their fishing gear with the camp owners until next year. These people sure get carried away with all this dri-ki stuff. We get some funny ones here now and again. Hey, you're not going to pick up some of this stuff too, are you? Gee!"

So you see, it makes no matter from what state you come or in what state your mind is, it's a fact that one kind of dri-ki nut is just as bad as another kind of dri-ki nut!

Before you start looking down your nose, just you try and gather a few pieces of dri-ki or driftwood and then see if you can leave it at that. Chances are, just picking up one piece will get you hooked. Think nothing of it! Notice how much nicer your waistline looks than those of the people giving you a critical eye. All this bending, stooping and stretching is an additional bonus for you. Now you have the best looking waistline and you have the waste to thank for it. Worthy compensation all around.

LET IT BEGIN WITH ME

It is easy to be wise after the event.
—English proverb

I CHATTED WITH A local clerk the other day, who had just returned from a visit to England. Our conversation centered on stores in that country.

"I went shopping in a neighborhood market one day and found they do things differently there," he said.

"For instance," I responded.

"Well, I had my groceries at the counter and the clerk rang them up. I gave her my money and she handed me the change. I waited for the groceries to be bagged, but she did nothing. Finally, she asked me what else I wanted. I, of course, told her I needed them put in something for me to carry away. 'Oh,' she told me, 'you put them in your own sack!' I didn't have my own 'sack,' so she told me she would give me one, but I would have to pay for it."

"That's a great idea," I answered. "We should do that right here. About time we began inconveniencing ourselves to overcome the trash problem."

"It will take a lot of education before such a step is

accepted," he responded.

"We could start right here in this store," was my naive rejoinder.

"I don't know about that. We were out of plastic bags one day a few weeks ago and we took a lot of heat!"

Jeepers, how about that. What great difficulty would it be to pop a canvas shopping bag in the car to tote home the groceries each week? Come to think about it, what *do* you do with the paper bags after you have unloaded the groceries? Do the bags go into the trash, or get folded and packed away in a cupboard until you can't close the door? What happens to them next? What if you didn't have the disposition of them to worry you—wouldn't life be simpler? Wouldn't there be less trash for the collector to carry off?

Perhaps the landfills wouldn't get so quickly filled. Maybe the groceries wouldn't cost as much if the grocer didn't have to buy paper bags in such quantity. And we are talking here about paper, a biodegradable product that will, over time, break down. Not so, plastic.

Plastic is another whole ball game. Plastic wrap around our meat. Dual-packed margarine. Toothbrushes locked in a plastic container openable only by Superman. Plastic, plastic, plastic. And this does not even include styrofoam, about which we have all read more than we want to hear.

It's simplistic, I know, but we must begin thinking about things we can do. We can't, as individuals, clean up the rivers, or stop corporations from raping the rain forests. That has to be left to governments and environmental agencies. But I am convinced that you and I can make a difference.

We can begin today, for instance, to limit the wanton waste of our water supply. Every member of the family showering and shampooing daily is ridiculous. Not only do we waste water, we deprive our bodies of much of their natural oils. This then results in our spending many dollars buying replenishing moisturizers and lubricants wrapped in layers of paper cartons under hermetically sealed plastic to bring our skin back to the "kind you love to touch."

My dear mother often said, "We grow weaker and wiser." I thought that a rather dumb old saw. But I begin to see there is much wisdom in it.

What can each of us do? In the words of that poignant song, "Let there be peace on earth, and let it begin with me."

GRANDMA GETS THE VIP TREATMENT

We tire of those pleasures we take,
but never of those we give.
　　　　　　　—J. Petit-Senn

I F YOU WOULD LIKE the formula for becoming a VIP—if only for half an hour—have I got news for you. Visit your 18 year old, staff-counselor granddaughter at a Maine summer camp. You are bound to come away impressed with the warmth and interest young people from around the world shower on you.

I know what I'm talking about, because I did just that one lovely July afternoon. This was Heather's first break with family before she packed off to a Baltimore college in August. Because I live only a dozen miles from Camp Med-O-Lark in Washington, Maine, I decided to visit and assure her she wasn't being forgotten. Truth is, I was anxious to see for myself how she was adjusting to the new situation of being a teacher rather than a student. Let me tell you, this mature young lady had everything under control.

I arrived at a lively moment. 400 campers and staff from all parts of the United States and many foreign countries can set a place a-buzz at any time, but mail time is pandemonium.

"I got a letter!" "Tom, there's a letter for you, come running!" "At last, *mail!*" Such shouts rang through the youthful community. How eagerly awaited is news from home. Along the way I met a man I suspected was camp owner, Neal Goldberg.

"Hello, are you Neal Goldberg?"

"No, I'm Ricky Silverman, a former camp counselor. I'm now in business in Philadelphia," Mr. Silverman explained, "but find a reason to come back each year, if only for a couple of days. I need a Maine 'fix'—a get-away to smell the pines and listen to the water lap against the boats."

After several offers of help from people along the way, I spotted the blonde Perry lady in a circle of counselors.

I chatted with campers from Texas, Florida, Virginia, London and Denmark as I waited for Heather's meeting to break up. Every conversation impressed me. They were brimming over with curiosity— where was I from, why was I there, was I staying? It was such a pleasant way to meet people, who were just as interested in me as I was in them. This is why I say that you too could be a very important person under similar circumstances.

Once Heather and I had spent her rest hour together and had walked the entire camp, it was time to let her go back to work. Heather was teaching pottery and jewelry-making, two artistic skills she refined during her senior year at Mount Blue High School in Farmington.

Before leaving I stopped in to speak with the camp director and tell him how impressed I was with his facility.

"Your comments please me," he said. "It's trite to say, but we hope the campers will be able to focus on other people as easily as they do on themselves while they are here. We trust the experience will allow them to see the bigger world, a world that's different from the place where they have spent the first 15 years or so of their lives."

Another aspect of the camp impressed me. At each cabin, in the flower garden, in the dance studio, in the most unexpected places, art was on display. A stained glass window in the office, an exquisite batik hanging, a wood sculpture in the garden, each perfectly placed. I mentioned this to the director.

He smiled, and said, " We offer a variety of classes in many aspects of art and craft, and we want our campers to see how effective such pieces can be in their daily lives."

As I drove the tree-shaded, dirt road from the camp, a multitude of positive feelings accompanied me. How fortunate Heather was to spend her summer in such a superb place. How stimulating for her to create a unique friendship with London-born Kat, the dance instructor, and Laura, the stunning young camper from Dallas, whose schedule is part of Heather's responsibility. And further, how lucky I was to have such a lovely child (as she will always be in my eyes) to visit in such a primeval place.

Maine is noted for the varied camping experiences it offers young people. The Maine Campers Association lists places that specialize in athletics, the arts, water skills, or environmental studies. A two or four-week summer camp experience offers a first, important, supervised step away from home for the fortunate young people able to participate.

Equally fortunate is the grandparent who can share a few hours of time at such an idyllic spot with a grandchild.

A TABLECLOTH'S JOURNEY

A creative economy is the fuel of magnificence.
—Ralph Waldo Emerson,
"Aristocracy"

T HE STORIES OF courageous women too often go unrecorded. It will not be so with Brone Raupiere. The story of her determination, artistic talent and love will be preserved, if only on these pages.

Brone Raupiere was born more than a century ago in a small Lithuanian village near the German border. Hers was a hard-working farm family who provided their own food, clothing, fuel and what little leisure activity they had time for. Hard work was constant and expected. This lively young lady spent her free time as other young women did, on needlework of every kind. Brone, however, had an exceptional gift for color and design.

During World War I this talented artist and her sister were forced to do road work in an area between the German and Russian armies. As the Germans advanced the Tsarist troops retreated, sweeping the Lithuanians into their work crew as they went. Brone was separated from her village, her family and her small daughter. She spent two years in Siberia, with only the consolation of knowing that her child was being cared for by her parents. At the close of the Bolshevik Revolution she was allowed to leave St. Petersburg and return to Lithuania.

Brone's health had become fragile, and her skill with needle and thread proved a life saver. She found work teaching at the local school. Sewing was a necessity in that era, and Brone knew her subject well. Not only did she teach others but she sharpened her own skills.

Family stories tell how close Brone and her daughter grew. Their readjustment after years of absence was difficult, and there were many turnings in their relationship, but the love between them was strong and steadfast.

Sometime in the 1920's a postcard design caught Brone's eye and she decided to enlarge it and use it in a piece of needlework. It was a trailing vine of grapes and leaves, subtly shaded, an effect harder to produce with thread than paint. The difficulty of the project was a challenge to her skill. She settled on a plan to transfer the succulent green grapes and twining grape leaves into a design for a wide border on the linen cloth. She then carefully selected the right colors to embroider the design on what she knew would be a table cover for her daughter.

Brone chose linen woven from Lithuanian flax, probably in a village kitchen similar to hers. The working floss was cotton, many colors of it, imported from Germany. Silk, Brone said, would not wash well, nor would it last as long as cotton. The cloth was 90 by 72 inches, a covering for a large table.

More than three years were spent on the piece, in what time Brone could spare. The close work greatly impaired her eyesight. By the end of her life she was blind.

Once the needlework was completed, Brone washed the piece, and ironed it while it was still wet. It was now firm enough so that all the interlacing segments could be cut away. This stage of the project was as exacting as the needlework. Every small strand of linen had to be removed leaving only the worked connecting strands in place.

By the mid 1930's the clouds of war were again threatening eastern Europe. Brone's daughter had married well and had given her three grandchildren. Her family was still intact, but facing an uncertain future.

When the Communists invaded her village Brone knew it was time to leave. With daughter and grandchildren she fled, packing her tablecloth among their few belongings. Her family agreed: the tablecloth would go with them.

Haven was found in East Germany, but not for long. They moved on to Free Germany after the war came to an end, and it was there a fateful event made passage to North America possible.

The Red Cross gave a pair of shoes to Brone. In the side of one shoe was the name of the Canadian woman who had sent the footwear. Being a gracious lady, Brone wrote a card of thanks to her benefactor. The Canadian woman was also Lithuanian, and was so astounded by the fateful communication, she contacted a Catholic organization, pledging sponsorship for the displaced family. Their next trip was across the Atlantic, and the linen tablecloth was one of the first things packed for the voyage.

Between 1948 and 1962 the family moved to the Chicago area where Brone managed a small rooming house/boarding home for fellow displaced Lithuanians. Her granddaughter, Violetta, went to Chicago schools and became a registered nurse. She married Albertas Aviza, a young

Lithuanian doctor who had grown up in Brone's village! In fact, the couple met at Brone's dinner table.

In 1964 Brone, Violetta and Albertas and their four children came to the V.A. Hospital at Togus. They moved into a house next to the Perry family and our children became playmates. The adult Avizas were warm, wonderful friends and Brone was a joy. They invited our whole family to share a traditional Lithuanian Christmas feast with them that took place right after Midnight Mass.

Brone's tablecloth made the occasion especially festive. It was during that midnight meal that the story of the travels of that beautiful piece of linen was told. A story full of love and wonder.

Brone Raupiere refused to leave behind the part of herself wrapped up in a few yards of Lithuanian linen and miles of cotton thread. She kept it beside her in times far more difficult than most of us could envision. Her former life was worked into that fabric, a life she refused to forget.

Today Brone is gone. I have lost touch with the Avizas, but I know wherever Violetta, Albertas, and their children are, Brone is still an integral part of their family. Her story and her work of art remain.

ISLAND ROOTS

You won't know why, and you
Can't say how
Such a change upon you came,
But—once you have slept on an island
You'll never be quite the same!
—Rachel Field

 HAVE A PHILOSOPHY —not scientific or based on statistical data—that people born of island parents have an affinity for land completely surrounded by water. Fact or fiction, I simply know I feel better and have a higher degree of perception and creativity when I am on an island. I gladly give credit for this to Elizabeth Leet, my mother, who was born in Economy, Nova Scotia, and John Luke, my father, who was born in Freeland Lot 11, Prince Edward Island.

Bernie and I often headed north when we found "keepers" for our four boys. It was to PEI, to Tignish, Alberton and the North Cape. He loved this land and found great joy in meeting hundreds of Perrys in Tignish! Often as we boarded the boat that carried us back to mainland Canada, we talked of buying a piece of land where both our fathers had been sired. Alas, that never happened during his lifetime.

My oldest son, John, called me one day—oh, that must be seven years ago— and said, "Mom, why don't we take a trip to PEI?" I was delighted. We asked the other boys and Paul was also free to take this junket with us. It was late March, very cold, and with a blizzard to clutter up our trip. We settled in with Jessie Graham, a remote cousin whose existence I discovered quite by accident a dozen years ago. Jessie is a native and her knowledge of PEI, its history and places, was invaluable to us outlanders. She was a treasure. Took us under her wing and regaled us all day and most of the night with stories and fables most wondrous to hear.

There were a couple of bachelor brothers who, it was said, were anxious to sell off a bit of land near the sand banks along Conroy Narrows. Themselves were not sure, when we got to them to talk about a purchase, if they wanted to sell, if they did, how much would they let go, or what price to ask for whatever they could part with, or if they would part with any at all! It was soon obvious we couldn't wait around an age for these gentle old fellers to come to a decision.

"Ah, let's be off with them. We'll find another place for you," Jessie said. And true to her word, she found us a place on Kildare Capes. A large red sign indicated there were two acres for sale. "I know the man who has that for sale. He has a blueberry business on the other side of the road. We'll call him as soon as we get home."

We walked the land with Mr. MacRae and looked over the ice-covered bay in a biting gale. He promised to hire a crew to fill in an abandoned cellar hole where a farmhouse had once stood. We agreed to be back in early May to sign papers and to finalize the transaction. Somehow I felt Bernie would be pleased that once again his heirs would take root on the island. I was overjoyed to know I finally owned a small piece of Canada and on an island at that.

For two years each son and his family came to the

island and camped out. In a mobile home or a tent—they savored the cliffed land and felt the tug strong enough to build a permanent shelter.

During my time in Belize with the Peace Corps, my son, John Perry, negotiated with Tignish carpenter/contractor, John Perry to put up a simple frame building. It was quickly done and photos of grandchildren romping about the shore reached me in my Caribbean home. I could hardly wait to see it.

The place is basic. Nothing pretentious at all. In fact, the first fall, vandals came by, took the front door, the lavatory and toilet and little else. Enough to discourage bringing any family heirlooms to the place. We pump water and use that to flush the toilet, and to wash the dishes in the sink and hand wash whatever clothes must be washed. No showers. It may be the only way my grandchildren will ever know the satisfaction of working to perform the daily acts of living that machines too often perform for us. I suspect they return home from a visit seeing life in a new and different fashion.

Once the cottage was built and I had taken up summer residence, Jessie asked me, "When you coming home to stay, Katy?"

"There's no reason why I'm not there, there are just too many commitments in the way," I would answer.

After several such conversations she told me, "Call that cottage 'No reason' and perhaps you'll think about it and get yourself here and stay awhile."

She's right. Perhaps I will.

ALL THE MILK
THEY WANT

*Katy and I used to scramble to get the
crystallized frozen cream that jutted
far above the milk bottle in winter.*
—John Luke

ILK HAS ALWAYS been an important
part of my diet. I could write pages
about it—from the family cow we
named Africa, to Johnny Galvin drop-
ping off a daily quart for the impover-
ished Luke family, the gift of an anonymous friend. Ah, yes, there is a lot of
milk in my background. As absurd as it sounds, let me share
a couple of thoughts on this amazing bovine product.

A fine Irish dentist had arrived in Millinocket about
the time I was born. Do you think I am going to tell you the
year? Indeed, I am: it was 1920. Dr. Harrigan married a local
girl and they produced two beautiful daughters. The family
raised show dogs. I was called to baby-sit the two youngsters
when Mama, Papa and the dogs attended weekend shows.

I loved going to the Harrigans. Being the family of a
professional man, you know, they lived *far* on the other side
of the tracks from where I lived with my mother and brother.
The Harrigans had a cupboard filled to overflowing with great
things to eat, and Mrs. H. always left cooked food for us. In

addition, they had lots of *milk!*

The girls were good kids and easy to care for. My surprise was at their indifference to milk. I remember walking them down to visit with my mother one afternoon.

"How are the girls doing, dear?" she asked.

"Oh, they're fine, Mom, but you know something— They have all the milk they want, and they don't drink any of it!"

Mother often told this story, yet not for a moment would I have you think the Lukes were hungry. Never. We did, however, hanker after more milk than we were able to acquire.

Many people today collect bottles and some even specialize in milk bottles. Do you remember the glass bottles with paper stoppers? The quart bottles were washed and put outside the door for the milkman to collect when next he appeared. We rarely bought pints of milk. The pints and half-pint bottles were usually for cream. Cream forty or fifty years ago wasn't expensive and was used pretty lavishly. Yet we weren't nearly as obese as today's population is, on synthetic cream.

Those milk bottles left on Maine doorsteps during the winter months are another story. If they weren't pulled into the house right after delivery, the tops would freeze and cream would pop far above the mouth of the container. The projecting cream (which came to the top, you know) took on comical shapes as the crystals froze and expanded. And what a delightful treat, to pull the paper top away and scoop a dollop of that frozen cream right into your mouth! I loved it.

Mother, once the cream had thawed, would pour it off and save it. We drank creamless milk, never thinking the future would hold special categories of 1% and skim milk. Our milk wasn't homogenized, so the cream and milk could be separated as we wished.

When I went to North Whitefield in the summer to visit our Tobin cousins I was always intrigued with the handling of milk from the family cow. Bert, the oldest brother, would brink in steaming pails of milk from the barn. Aunt Libby would take her meticulously cared-for piece of cheese-cloth, place it securely over the lip of the milk pail, and strain the milk into shallow, round tins. These were whisked down to the cool, damp cellar. Quick cooling was important. Yesterday's "sets" would be brought back up, and the cream scraped away.

At the end of the week the accumulated cream (what was left from multiple ice cream churnings and whipped cream puddings) was allowed to stay in a warm place and churned into butter. Now that was an operation.

Aunt Libby almost boiled her hands before she touched the newly coagulated butter. She rinsed the mass in dozens of washes of clear, cold water, squeezing and kneading it to eliminate all the buttermilk. Once confident it was clear, she salted it liberally, made it into an appropriate size, and wrapped it in wax paper before returning it to the cool cellar.

The buttermilk was drunk, and ended up also in buttermilk biscuits and several other delicacies only Aunt Libby knew how to make.

With all that milk available, I was again amazed that the Tobin kids rarely drank it! Brother John and I got all we wanted when we visited that loving farm family.

My goodness, all this chatter about milk has done it. I think there's just about a glass of the stuff left in the refrigerator to accompany a delicious molasses cookie. Milk, anyone?

KRIS—BOUND FOR THE USSR

I doubt I'll ever remember anything as long as
my five weeks with Russian kids this summer.
—Kristin Perry, 15

S I WRITE THIS it's late June, 1990. In just four days my third grandchild, Kris, will join other teenagers from around the country for an evening of sociability and orientation before a five week stay in the Soviet Union. She is one of more than 80 participating in the peace camp initiated by the Samantha Smith Foundation in Hallowell. After that one evening it's off to Russia.

Shortly after Samantha's book of adventures in Russia was published I asked Jane Smith to have Samantha sign it for Kris. Even at that time I felt a kinship between these two young ladies. In my subconscious I nurtured the idea that Kris might follow Samantha's lead. Now it is to be.

It was last winter that a newspaper from the Foundation arrived in my mail. I read about the proposed 1990 camp, and the idea popped into my head— what an opportunity for Kris. I looked long and hard at my meager bank book, then called Kris's parents.

It had to be their decision, of course, whether she

would fly away in June with the group or not. Once the decision had been made and the young lady was asked her pleasure, there was no turning back. Kris has devoted all her spare time during the past six months to learning everything possible about Russian politics, culture, music and language. I think she is well prepared for the journey. Over the past weeks she has been gathering every sort of small, lightweight article that says "Maine." These will be gifts for the Russian young people she lives with during her stay. I am told she will bring back small mementos from them as well.

The itinerary begins with one evening in Boston to meet other campers and chaperones. The flight to the USSR puts them down in Leningrad, I think, where they'll spend a week with a host family. Then it's off to a camp on the shores of the Black Sea. The final week will again be with a family, this time in Moscow. She then flies back to Boston to the arms of her devoted family—more mature, yet, hopefully, the same shy, simple, no-nonsense, lovable Kris. She will have experienced an opportunity for growth and maturity too priceless to calculate.

The world grows smaller with each passing decade. We know instant gratification and far more about the world than we did even last year. What we need to know is that, as a species, we are more alike than unlike. We must realize that customs are different but people all have the same emotions, the same likes and dislikes, the same moods and worries. An extremely valuable realization when you are 15, before you have firmed up your views of the world.

Travel is a fine way to learn, and although five weeks is hardly long enough to absorb another way of life, it is a beginning, a beginning that is more easily made in youth. I would love to think I can do a similar thing for each of the other grandchildren—but at last count that runs to eight more! At any rate, I will savor the adventure almost as much as Kris, when she recounts her stories to me on her return. It will be far more absorbing than a travel book. What could be nicer?

So, dear Kris, fly away and have fun, and gather every possible memory before you come home to us in Maine.

A GIFT TO BE SIMPLE

He gives only the worthless gold
Who gives from a sense of duty.
　　　　　—James Russell Lowell,
　　　　　"Vision of Sir Lancelot"

RUTH CALLED A FEW DAYS AGO and invited me to lunch. Her husband was off at their far-away camp and she was hungry for some woman-talk. I was flattered to be the second half of the conversation. The lunch was delightful and I came home sated with good food, warm thoughts of this beautiful, 82-year-old lady, and bearing a bowl of bulbs.

As I cleaned the kitchen of breakfast things this morning, I thought about Ruth and her generosity. On the window ledge over the sink a low green dish is dwarfed by tall green shoots of paper narcissus that hourly are being topped by small white flowerets centered with a quartet of yellow dots. This oasis, breathing spring into the early winter morning, is a welcome sight. Such a simple thing—three brown bulbs bursting forth—but what a feast for eyes now tuned to leafless trees and dull lawns outside.

I promised Ruth I would return the ceramic dish once the blossoms passed, but she quickly turned the idea aside.

"I don't care a bit about the dish, but I would love to have the pebbles back. They are hard to find, especially at this time of year. They came from our camp up north and I really treasure them," she told me.

You can be sure the pebbles will go back to Ruth's cozy kitchen, where an ever-constant wood stove bakes small pots of beans. Ruth, you see, treks about the neighborhood carrying these small pots to neighbors who live alone, or who do not have the luxury of a constant source of oven heat as she does. Even if she didn't have the stove, I strongly suspect the lady would find ways of brightening her neighborhood.

Nor am I done with my tale of this lovely lady and her man. There was a knock at my front door yesterday. When I answered it, there was Ruth's husband toting a ten gallon container full of crystal clear water.

"Brought this back from camp, Katy," he said. "Runs right into the camp, gravity feed. Great drinking water. Ruth suspected you'd like a taste."

This is a man of well-chosen comments devoid of flowery embellishments. He refused an invitation for lunch and turned away to where his canoe-laden truck waited.

I brought the container into the house and immediately poured a glass of water. Ambrosia. During the day I consumed several glasses, and savored its goodness and the thoughtfulness of the giver with every drop.

Lately I've been immersed in the glorious music of Aaron Copeland, who used one of the Shaker communities' lovely tunes in one of his compositions. " 'Tis a Gift to be Simple" in the inimitable Copeland musical rendition has been much in my mind. As I enjoyed the touch of life in Ruth's gift of flowers and drank deeply from her husband's gift of water, I was moved to unite these two moments in my life.

Simple gifts, gifts from the hands and hearts of uncomplicated Maine people—yes, I will say it with all tenderness, simple people.

How blessed I am to be included in the circle of people who share their simplicity and friendship with me.

AGE SEES THINGS
DIFFERENTLY

Extraordinary how potent cheap music is.
—Noel Coward

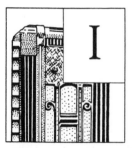 VISITED MY FATHER in Camden one weekend when I was in college. That was about 1939, and Frank Sinatra was the love of every young lady's life. His voice was absolutely lovely, so we thought, and the stuff that dreams are made of. I know I was not alone in my silent adoration. To be sure, de Bingo (Bing Crosby, for those newcomers to the pop music scene) was hot stuff at the time, but Frankie was just emerging as the idol of the airwaves.

We were not wired to constant walkmen or boom boxes then, often didn't even have a radio in our dormitory rooms, but we coveted the sound of this guy's music.

That weekend I discovered that my father, who *had* a radio and could listen as often as he wished, didn't wish— he killed the sound! His distaste for the music Sinatra sang was unfeigned and profound. He was terribly unkind, I thought, when he criticized.

"Can't for the life of me see why you kids swoon over that guy. His music is terrible," he would say.

In spite of his comments, perhaps, in part, because of them, I remained a passionate follower of Frank's style.

It was a decade or two later when a British group was introduced by the laconic Ed Sullivan. The Beatles took off like a well-fueled rocket and yes, you guessed it, I was not impressed. By this time, you see, I had a brood of growing kids of the age group which almost—oh, let's face it, did—worship those Cockney guys. I tolerated the music, I think, better than my father had my earlier idol, but I was not won over.

Life goes on, and the issue of accepting or not accepting music lagged far behind the effort of keeping the boys in "sneakers and BandAids," as my husband used to say. One evening, however, while I was listening to the radio in front of the wood-burning kitchen range, I tuned in to the Boston Pops under the effective baton of Arthur Fiedler. The concert included several numbers composed by non other than the Beatles ensemble. What an awakening!

The melodies were hauntingly beautiful. I immediately questioned the source, but they were truly compositions dreamed up by that unique group. You know the rest. I rethought my prejudice.

There is a lesson here, methinks. We tolerate, and even more, enjoy the things we know. The unknown is often unacceptable. I don't know why that is, but I suspect it's a fact.

Listening to the radio this morning—you see, I now have one of these contraptions in *every* room, no less—I heard a promotion for a world-wide concert Sinatra is scheduled to make. The program traced the changes in his tone, delivery and voice over the past—what is it—six decades! No doubt about it, his is not the clear, melodic sound of even twenty years ago, but he still belts out a song so you get goose bumps. For the over-60s the bumps may be the result of long-submerged memories evoked by his singing, but even the younger people used to today's repetitious beat just might like what they hear. At any rate, the promotion sent me into a random travel down memory lane.

I was transported to tea dances in the rec' room at UMF's Purington Hall, to a country weekend dance in nearby Jefferson, to lonely nights during World War II when I shed many tears to Sinatra's music—music I had listened to with my Pacific-bound husband. Music does have the capacity to send me into reverie, although it may be memory of pathos.

The music of Sinatra, I guess, is as much a part of me as my knitting or baking. I am moved to dance with it, sing with it, sway or cry with it, depending on how it stirs me. Does music do this to you? I often think I could do without art or books, not easily, but easier than I could live without music.

I wonder, if my father were alive today would he finally come around to thinking better of the music Old Blue Eyes makes? I hope he would, for that was a precious time in his life too.

OVERCOME BY LIQUID

The terrible fluidity of self-revelation
—Henry James,
The Ambassadors

 WAS IN the Whitefield pool for my tri-weekly swim when the phone rang. Pat, the owner, left me in mid-sentence to make the long dash into the adjoining house before the caller gave up. Almost immediately she came back with an alarming statement: "Get your a- - out of there, Katy. That was the Hallowell police. The Kennebec is about to overflow Water Street. If you and Judy have things in that store of yours that will be spoiled by the flood, you got to make tracks, lady." Pat doesn't mince words.

It took me a minute to realize the spring rains had created what we hoped would never be enough water to necessitate removal of merchandise from our shop, Yankee Doodle. But I believed what Pat said and I pulled myself out of the water and grabbed a towel.

The first order of business was to alert my business partner, Judy. Fortunately, she was near a phone. "Get a truck and a couple pair of hands," I told her, "and meet me at the store. We've had a red alert to vacate Yankee Doodle before the river washes it away!"

No time, I realized, to dry sodden tresses or go home for a cup of coffee and toast. No time to change from the beat-up sweatsuit I donned when I got out of bed on pool days.

I grabbed my fleecy jacket and pulled an old watch cap over wet hair to help fend off the sharp, early spring cold. It was hard to envision what I would find when I drove the 15 miles from the pool to Hallowell, but things looked better than I expected. The water was lapping up the bank between the Wharf and Renaissance Framers, but had not reached the street level, so far. Predictions still maintained the street would be under water before noon.

I had just unlocked the door when Judy walked in with her husband and two stalwart male friends in tow. Their pickup truck was parked by the front door.

No one issued any orders, as I remember. Each sensed what was most perishable—cotton place mats, paper posters, delicate pottery, wooden boxes. For over two hours we packed items into boxes and the men packed the boxes into the truck. We realized the bigger things would have to stay. Things we could not pack away or load into the truck were stashed as high off the floor as possible. It would be an unusual flood if those wares were watered down.

By the time we felt confident we had done everything we reasonably could to prevent disaster, Judy and I, the men, and Pat, who had appeared with her pickup as reinforcement, were hungry, cold and exhausted.

"Come on, you two," Pat ordered—she has the personality of a female top sergeant—"Let's get down to Slate's and have an Irish coffee, guaranteed to chase away the chills and put red blood back in your veins."

Who would *dare* deny that order? We gave a last look at our work, knowing we had a lot of taking and putting back to do once the water receded, then locked the door and headed south.

Slates was mobbed. Lots of other merchants and willing helpers had been hard at work too. In addition, there were lots of onlookers waiting to see the foibles of Miss Kennebec (a river is feminine, isn't it?).

"Let's see, there are four of us. Make it four Irish coffees, please," Pat said, as she tipped back in her chair to reach for her billfold in her back pocket.

At this point it is necessary to add a few words about this indomitable woman. Pat is bossy, more than ordinarily capable, and generous beyond all reason. When she tips back in her chair and reaches for her greenbacks, she almost slaps other hands that make the same gesture. Over the years we have learned it does absolutely no good to argue with the likes of this one. On the morning of the flood none of us even thought to. We were probably too pooped to try.

We began sipping the steaming brew and slowly my hands regained feeling. It had not yet reached my feet, though. Across the way we chatted with others and compared the situation as we saw it. In this way, the cup lowered.

I left to speak with a friend in the next room. When I returned the trio was waiting for me. I sat down to another steaming cup, more, far more than I needed, but, as I said, my feet were still wet and cold.

More time elapsed and a dim fog settled over me. When I realized a third (!) cup of the black magic sat in front of me, I began to protest.

"Drink that, Katy, or you'll have your death!" the prophet offered. I did as I usually do, and obeyed Pat's orders.

Morning was swiftly turning into afternoon and still we sat. After three generous libations, I realized time had not allowed for solid food. Well, perhaps it had been inclination rather than *time*. At any rate, I was not so far gone that I didn't know I should have stopped while my feet were wet and cold. I should have more forcefully refused the third cuppa'—and hoped I was counting right.

We started back toward the shop. We had passed the magic hour. High noon had come and gone and the water was no longer rising. It was such a relief I sat right down on the curb and stretched my feet into the street. A friend drove me home.

Some time later I was having lunch at a Hallowell cafe. Judy was with me and we spoke with the ladies at the next table (we do this a lot, you see).

One of them said, "I think the last time I saw you, Katy, was the day the water was coming over the main street, back in '84. You were sitting on the curb looking across at Yankee Doodle, and I must say, you were a sorry sight!"

She was being polite. I was a bedraggled witch by that time. At almost any given moment I can make a perfect fool of myself. And it's even easier filled with several hot cups of coffee laced with clear, amber, Irish whiskey.

Note: Fortunately for all concerned, during the major flood of 1987, when Hallowell's Water Street was truly under water, I was out of the country and away from any temptation to swim, salvage shop merchandise, or imbibe Irish coffee!

COPING

*To understand is hard. Once
one understands, action is easy.*
—Sun Yat-Sen

OMEONE ONCE ASKED how one copes with being a widow. I've thought about that a lot. You could answer glibly, "The best you can." That, however, is unsatisfactory.

Thinking *me* after 37 years of thinking *we* is never easy, even when the woman has been in business for a decade and is quite capable of making decisions as a single person. Going home at night to a house where no one else eats with you, or, more barren, sleeps with you, quickly makes home feel like nothing more than a house. Communication is nonexistent. The radio or television is a darn poor substitute for a human being across the table, someone with whom to share the woes and joys of the day.

The tired adage, though, does ring true—things get better. You adjust. Well, you adjust if you work at it. It might seem natural to wear a frown and grieve long, seeking solace and concern from family and friends. Time must and should be given to adjusting to this new part of your life.

A caution, though. If such a period goes on too long (and I have seen this, but worked tremendously hard to prevent it in myself) you find the temptation is to indulge in self pity. Bad, really bad. Such a tendency catches on easily and before you know it, you are not the kind of independent person you hope to be, but a self-centered one . One, let's face it, unlikely to be invited to neighborhood gettogethers. For most families, almost without exception, have dark aspects to their lives and refrain from adding another cloud to their horizon.

So what do you do? Of course there's no magic formula. Many will not live out their days solo. Often another man comes along, one with whom you share common interests and you form another relationship. That's fine. There are those of us, however, who are intimidated by such a prospect.

Being single isn't all that bad, once you've gotten comfortable with your new state in life. That may seem like sour grapes on my part. I have only had one offer of marriage in my nine years of widowhood and that was from an 82 year old Peace Corps Volunteer six years ago. So that option was never a viable one for me. I fear I've found too much to recommend being single to be tempted.

I have been fortunate in finding exciting, rewarding things to do. I have taken a grandchild on a two-week horse and wagon trek into the Greek Peloponnesos, have joined a young lady friend for a visit and tour of Ireland, have operated a craft business, spent two years as a Peace Corps Volunteer, watched grandchildren (at my own terms—short terms!), done extremely interesting volunteer work, and spent many hours at my typewriter turning personal thoughts into columns and books.

If I have any advice, any how-to for a recently bereaved woman, it would be, casual as it sounds, to get on with your life. The door has closed on the previous phase of your time and all that remains are the wonderful memories. You'll never lose them. The house may burn, the memories remain. You may marry again, but the good times from the other life will stay.

Shut off the TV. Don't, for the love of all that's holy, get hooked into an hour or (God forbid) several hours a day with that consuming instrument. Not only does it waste your time, it stifles your thinking. You are living someone else's life, when you could be out doing great things yourself.

Something I once wrote elicited the response, "But Katy, people *do* remember the bad things in life. Everyone doesn't remember only the good."

That's true, and I admit to presenting only *my* point of view, for that's the only one I know. But if you dwell on the unpleasant and let it dominate your view of life, and, worse yet, intrude on your communication with others, you are doing yourself a great disservice.

Attitude is crucial. Learn to rely on yourself. Learn to balance your own checkbook (I have rarely *ever* been able to do this without outside help, yet I remain solvent). Learn to call in the plumber when leaks begin under the kitchen sink. Ask a neighborhood child to shovel your path. Learn to make one-dish meals, but continue to invite other friends, including male friends, to join you now and then for dinner. Use the best china, light the candles. The genuine heck with what the neighbors think. You are completely in charge of your life and you can jolly well live it as you see fit.

The library has books, dozens of them, on ways to improve your feelings of self-worth. Read these books, digest the logic between the covers. The test, though, is putting the suggestions to work. Decide that you will get up every morning thanking God (whatever your God is) that you are alive, and get out and do something. Make a plan for *every* day. Walk to a neighbor, bake a cake, play a game of tennis, get a part-time job—do *something* outside the house. Get alive and begin to enjoy whatever time you have.

A pad of paper, a pencil and an eraser (yep, you'll make mistakes) is a good beginning. Start writing some of the good things you recall about the days long gone. Even silly little things such as the day the kids put the cat in the rain barrel to see if she could swim. You'll be amazed at how pleased your grown kids will be, that you remembered the event.

Some time back I said the bad memories fall away. They have for me, at least. Even those few I fail to release bring a kind of honing to the spirit. If I look closely at them I realize I grew and learned a great deal from adversities—I endured some difficult times and survived. They were and still are valuable aspects of a life already 70 years gone. I certainly haven't done everything right in my years of widowhood, but I am convinced I haven't done everything wrong, either.

In the words of the Chinese political leader Sun Yat-Sen, "To understand is hard. Once one understands, action is easy." Work hard to understand who you are. Then act.

ONE WAY
TO VOLUNTEER

As for him who voluntarily performeth a
good work, verily God is grateful and knowing.
—The Koran

T IS FLATTERING to be asked to serve on a library's board of trustees. Flattering in that people think you literate enough to serve, and additionally flattering to feel citizens believe you have something to contribute. So, of course, I accepted the invitation. As a duly installed member of the board of Hubbard Free Library in Hallowell, I am qualified, I believe, to tell you something of this fascinating building.

Truth is, it is not the building, as historic and charming as it is, that I would speak about. It's what the building contains—the contents of a long, unused museum and the collection of delicate, old and valuable books.

As the story goes, in the late 1800's, a wing was built onto the library to contain artifacts from local people who traveled the world bringing back amazing articles. The museum began to swell and soon ran out of both space and proper cataloging. Because it was also unheated, it was closed to the public during the cold winter months.

In the early part of the century, people became far more interested in the newfangled vehicle that Henry Ford and the Stanley brothers of Kingfield, Maine created and began to travel more widely, leaving the small museum often unattended and certainly uninteresting. For the next 50 years or so, the room was more or less forgotten.

In the late 1970's the trustees saw the need for more children's activities and reading materials. The decision was made to retrofit the museum as a children's center, complete with child-sized tables and chairs, and a comfy carpet with building toys to encourage kids to entertain themselves. Fresh, eye-level bookcases displayed the bright covers of new children's books to tempt small people's eyes.

The current board of trustees is most interested in analyzing the artifacts taken from the museum and stored in other parts of the library. Board president Gerry Mahoney asked if I would chair a committee to look at all the articles in the museum collection and inventory what was there.

There was absolutely no problem finding a dozen people from the community and surrounding towns and cities who were interested and willing to give a few hours a week to go through the accumulation of 100 years, list the objects, and in some manner identify them for the computer. It took about six weeks to complete the work which did not include the piles of old newspapers, or the collection of bound papers, and historic and valuable older texts.

The librarian and her staff have entered the hand-written lists in the computer. Now there's a working list from which a professional archivist, or historian can work. The volunteer committee did a magnificent job—a really valuable service to the library, Kennebec County, the state of Maine and future historians.

Where do we go from here? Good question. Future meetings of the Board must wrestle with this issue. Hopefully, a professional can be hired to go over the computer list and help make a determination about what is there, what pieces should remain in a library, what should be donated to museums—what, perhaps, even be scrapped (although this will be a really hard call).

Exciting? You bet. When you open a small document dated 1796 and find an official seal with the signature of Samuel Adams penned below, or a signed letter from Teddy Roosevelt or even a beautiful painting of scenes around Hallowell dated 1926—you know this is a building rich in historic legend, lore, and art.

Those who worked on the project sometimes felt like the man who fell upon the Comstock Lode in California—or the archeologist who found the Rosetta Stone in the Holy Land—such treasures under our fingertips—and we weren't really looking for such wondrous fare.

The next time you are invited to serve on a board, think twice before you say "no." You might have lots more fun giving your time than you realize. You will be making a valuable contribution when you volunteer and it's highly possible you will learn lots of things along the way and have fun doing it.

GEORGE TUCKER
A MAN OF FEW,
WELL-CHOSEN WORDS

*The peculiarity of the New England hermit
has not been his desire to get near to God,
but his anxiety to get away from man.*
—Hamilton Wright Mabier,
Backgrounds of Literature

 T WOULD BE FAR FROM the truth if I wrote of George Tucker as a man I know. What little I do know of him was learned in a brief half-hour visit at his blacksmith shop one lovely spring day. I can say with conviction, however, that George Tucker is both a New England "character" and a man of character. Our meeting was thus:

The day had grown warm and had cleared considerably since leaving home. Encouraged by the lovely weather, we had gone further afield than planned, and we found we were more than ready for food when the lunch hour arrived. It wasn't difficult to locate a country store and buy crackers and cheese and a cool drink to remedy our situation. The view we had reached was breathtaking. Neither of us wanted to eat even our modest repast in the confines of a car, so we drove on looking for a likely spot to stop.

The open door of a blacksmith shop seemed to yawn a welcome. We entered and greeted the smithy within, who kindly allowed us to walk to the crest of land behind his shop to enjoy the view and eat our lunch. He went a bit further and pointed out a well-used but unobtrusive path that would lead us to a comfy stone wall, where the vista was even more startling. Being well-brought up creatures, we returned after our lunch to thank our host for his hospitality. He called to us to come in and introduced himself as George Tucker.

Our noses led us to the rear of the shop where a fire was smoldering on the forge encouraged by hand bellows that the blacksmith motivated. Curiosity prompted us to ask what he was going and, perhaps sensing that our question was sincere, George told us he was making a couple of pins for his tractor. We watched the entire procedure and asked myriad questions.

With the completion of his task the talk eased around to something about George himself. Rather reluctantly he confided that he had been born about 85 years ago in the house just across the road, and that as a child, boy and man he had worked in this blacksmith shop, first with his grandfather, then his father, and finally alone.

"Have you always been a blacksmith?" I asked.

"No, for one year I worked on the Waterville-Lewiston electric car railroad."

"Didn't you like railroading, George?"

"Best G-- D--- job I ever had."

"Why did you leave it, then, after only one year? Were you unhappy away from home?"

"Whole railroad folded. Nothing to do but come home. Been here ever since. Was road commissioner for the town for about ten years, but gave that up a while back. My legs been bad. Fact, this is the first day I been here in the shop in over a year."

"There's a lot of pretty fancy modern machinery here, George. How come?"

"Made everything myself—some things out of stuff I bought, but most of it out of things I found here on the place. Got a homemade steam engine upstairs. Made the boiler myself—another feller sold me the engine. There are 14 half-inch high-pressure fire engine tubes in that boiler."

"Mind if we go up and see it?"

"Go ahead. Bad stairs, though—watch your head."

We ascended the stairs and found the steam engine. Took a minute or two, you can bet, being a couple of women who had never seen a real, steam engine before in our lives!

We called down to tell George it was pretty smart, and beheld him pulling himself, very carefully, up the sliver-sized stairs. He wanted to point out some other things since we were there, a lathe with wooden works, and a windmill he is currently working on. A large auger with two handles to give better purchase and that would drill a big hole, took my eye. I commented on it, and he explained what it was and showed us how it was used. It looked like just the thing to make an unusual lamp base, and I shyly asked,

"George, ever thought to sell any of these things?"

"Nope. Long as I live might need them. Don't care what happens after I finish."

No sale. No lamp.

It occurred to both my friend and me that quite possibly everything that had ever entered this shop was still here, unless it had been something brought in for repairs, or made for some special customer. The attic of this blacksmith shop would give Honest Ernie the antique dealer an itching ulcer.

When we finally became embarrassed with our own curiosity and fearful that dear George might feel we were trying to make inroads into his shop, we forced ourselves to descend. It was not easy. There were still hundreds of corners that we hadn't looked into yet. We both stood on the ground floor with our mouths open and our breaths held while George of the bad leg, propelled himself beautifully backwards down the stairs.

I told George I did a radio program and asked if he ever listened to the radio.

"News, that's about all I care for."

We left it at that!

We apologized for having kept the good man from his work, but George informed us that his sisters were probably waiting for him to come down to lunch anyway, and maybe he'd get back up later and finish the tractor pins.

"But your fire has gone out; that's a bother," I said.

"No bother, got nothing else to do. Can't even mow the lawn anymore with this bum leg. Got a young feller here helps the girls and me with the garden and the chores."

"How old are your sisters, George?"

"Being how they's women, don't think I should tell you their ages, but I'm their baby brother." The twinkle in his eye betrayed the fact that he was, indeed, pulling our leg.

"Please forgive us for keeping you away from your lunch so long, George, but may we come back another day and look at your view again?"

"Yep."

At this juncture there was some comment from George about his not being good for much these days and he didn't have much to offer the world. After this confession from him, which I suspect took a lot of courage, I had to comment.

"Without doubt there are many men with more fame and fortune and perhaps better health than you, George Tucker, but I'm willing to bet that many of them would give a pretty penny to wake up each morning and look on the peaceful and happy valley that you can see from your little old blacksmith shop!"

Looking just a bit touched, George agreed maybe there were such, he didn't know.

As we got back into the car, my friend and I both promised we would be back to call. Ever a ham I had to add, "George, be sure and keep your radio on, and some day you might hear me talking about your beautiful view." George, the man of few but well-chosen words, had the last one. His retort:

"Yep, if I happen to think of it!"

George Tucker had really impressed me, but you just know I didn't get to first base with him.

SHUN-PIKING

Travel East
Travel West
After all
Home's best
—Anonymous

HINK ABOUT IT—Maine has some spectacular vistas. Every county boasts some elevation where you can look out over the fields and woods and see almost into tomorrow. Over the years I have traveled about avoiding the major highways—shun-piking. In the process, I've sopped up some views that are indelibly etched on my memory. Let me tempt you with a few of the gems I have found.

If you start in the Kennebec County area, take route 27 south to Dresden. Just beyond the Texaco station there is a road on the left leading to Blinn Hill. It winds along and finally crests onto open terrain. Looking to your left you have spread out before you a panoramic picture of the river valley (both Kennebec and Eastern) that should make you pull over to the side to savor the beauty. An early evening ride to this height is well worth the time and effort it takes. I'm surprised how many local people have never seen that view.

Those who live in the Mount Vernon/Vienna region well know the road to Farmington. Along this way (route 41) you will be treated to several views of towering mountains in the distance. As wondrous as the view are the colors of the scene. In spring the soft purples, pinks, and blues bring a catch to your throat.

A few weeks ago I opted to come home from a family visit in Harrison via South Paris to Turner on route 117. There were spots that spring day, that wouldn't be visible later in the season for all the foliage. I could see for miles over lakes, valleys and the inevitable church spire. Again the colors would be the envy of an artist's palette.

The simple fact is, almost any ride in this wooded, watered, mountainous, sea-coastal state is enough to bring visitors in droves. It's sad we natives don't see some of the grandeur around us because we're in a catapulting hurry and opt to travel the congested major roadways. Let me urge you to pull off the arteries and coast along the roads less traveled (an interesting book by that name might pique your interest, too).

Many times we think it's imperative to spend lots of money, time and effort planning a trek to far places. I do not deny the extreme fun of such plans, but if life doesn't allow us to travel afar, there are still great places to discover in Maine. Just a couple more suggestions: looking at the back side of Mount Katahdin as you drive north on the interstate near Sherman; a short climb to Tip-Toe Mountain on Vinalhaven Island; a ride down route 16 from Abbot Village to Bingham; a sweeping view of the coast from Mount Batty in Camden; a walk around Mount Blue in Weld.

Do you know the Katahdin Iron Works out of Brownville Junction? Or coming out of the woods onto broad agricultural fields in Aroostook County? Or winding your way along the St. John River from Van Buren to Madawaska to Fort Kent? If you haven't experienced these easily accessible tours, you have rare treats in store.

Get out the map of Maine, plot some family adventures, travel light, and discover the riches we have right under our noses. One of the bonuses of such a trip is that there is almost certainly an ice-cream cone waiting along the way. What simplicity and what fun!

MEAT ON THE HOOF!

*Life in the country would be impossible
without neighbors!*
—Katy Perry

ODAY'S KIDS, ESPECIALLY those who live in the city, probably think pork chops or pork roasts grow in the meat counter of the supermarket. They might be amazed—or even traumatized—to find that those delicious cuts of meat are personally grown by the likes of Porky Pig or the charming Miss Piggy. It causes me to wonder sometimes how the reality of everyday life can best be introduced to these computer-wise youngsters.

Things were considerably different when my boys were young. They had first-hand experience with where meat came from. Take the time Ol' Dad and I squeezed out fifteen whole dollars to buy a piglet.

Our first major purchase was a cow. This holstein carried the exact shape of the continent of Africa on her side and was therefore, of course, referred to by that name. She was a good family bovine. Her twice-a-day offering provided plenty of milk for the four boys and an unknown number of barn kittens (that, darn it all, grew too quickly into cats.) We splurged with homemade ice cream, and I made butter at least twice a week. There was still a surplus and the sensible answer seemed to be—get a pig. A farmer down the road had advertised, "Spring piglet for sale, *cheap*." We found a grain bag, loaded the kids in the pick-up and trundled down the road.

Piglets are absolutely captivating! Every one of the kids wanted to hold the bag with the wiggling porker inside. They had such a great time during the ride it seemed a shame to deposit the little feller alone in the enclosure that had been prepared. We knew he would be lonesome without his piglet brothers and sisters for warmth and company, but reasoned that was how things had to be.

It turned out to be an especially cold and wet Spring. One day Bernie came into the house and announced, "That pig isn't eating. I think it has a cold, if not pneumonia. Katy, why don't you call the vet and if he can see the pig, you and John take him to Damariscotta this afternoon."

Just like that I got to be a pig-carer. How in heaven's name would we handle catching and confining that scrappy pig! Well, obviously experience wasn't a requirement because we managed the whole thing.

The diagnosis was that the poor little critter's solitary life had contributed to an advanced case of pneumonia. We came home with medication to be administered three times a day. Even this undertaking was carried out pretty well for amateurs. Soon our little porker was lapping up grain mixed with Africa's wholesome milk, and growing frisky and plump.

We took special pride, John and I, that we were able to handle this little animal's illness so well. In fact, we really became attached to him. I began to wonder how the boys would accept Mr. Pig's departure and what would be said when pork appeared on our dinner table.

Then a new event took place that for a while suggested our porker might depart a different way. Spring was slowly turning warm and friendly. Our animals were thriving and Piggy was hefty and pretty active. So active, that one morning Pete called, "Mom, look—Piggy is going down to see Mr. Bailey!" Sure enough, Piggy was rooting through the weeds along the fence between our property and the neighbor's. I was horrified. Our original payment and other expenses made this creature a sizable investment towards next winter's food budget—I had to catch him. Easier said than done.

I sneaked up and nearly caught his tail, but wasn't fast enough. I ran around him and tried in vain to head him back to our barn. I yelled to John and Pete to find a bag to put him in, should I ever be lucky enough to catch him.

Never mind a greased pig—have you ever thought *what* you would grab for in capturing a runaway pig? Not a lot of options, you know. After numerous misses, I ran back to the house and called Mr. Bailey.

It was like the rainbow after the rain when Mr. Bailey and a helper rounded the corner of the barn. There were two of them and they knew how to handle the situation. After my half hour of futile effort, those two men had Piggy in the burlap sack in mere minutes. Life in the country would be impossible without neighbors.

Yep, for sure my kids know where pork comes from, and how much work goes into getting it to the table. It was an exhausted, rattled mother who recounted the tale of the runaway pig to her husband that night.

I still think little pigs are about the most lovable creatures on the farm.

HOW "BUY" LOVE

Love sought is good,
but given unsought is better.
—Shakespeare,
Twelfth Night

A REMARK IN A LETTER written by Tennessee Williams, quoted in the book *Five O'Clock Angel*, once stopped me in my reading. Williams was expressing his remorse for not acting more kindly to a friend. "I put her on a plane—but I paid her expenses coming and going. It is much easier to give money than love..."

I put the paper down and did some honest-to-God soul searching. What a startling statement—and how it impacts on one's own life.

I found myself recalling dozens of instances when giving money soothed my guilt for not doing more. It is easier to give to the church building campaign than to put my shoulder to the proverbial wheel; easier, by far, to drop alms into the poor box than see the hungry and homeless all about; easier for a troubled conscience to send off a check to a home for wayward children and yes, easier to offer dollars to a cleanup-the-environment campaign than to expect me to take part in a wayside walk to clear the debris. The easy way out, that's the best way. It feels like the mentality of the age. Do you agree? Do you suffer the same pangs about the way you inhabit this place at this time?

I recalled a conversation I had recently with an old acquaintance. I'd been sitting in the office of a professional man, one I have seen for many years, chatting about our families. His son, an only son, had graduated from college, taken an apartment in the city and was working.

"The job isn't very satisfying, I guess," he said.

"But he *is* doing what he wishes, isn't he? I offered.

"Oh, I suppose so, but I think there is a lot of help from me that he looks for and expects."

"Yes, I know what you mean. It's hard to cut the ties, isn't it?" I suggested. "That may be the hardest thing we do, as parents, open the door of life and set them adrift, on their own. Alone to make their mistakes and learn from them. Right?"

The man looked at me and said, "Yes, that's a hard thing for a parent to do, Katy. Being strong and firm about cutting off the money from home is hard."

Perhaps you completely disagree. I might not have even thought about our conversation again if I hadn't read that remark by Tennessee Williams. Ah, yes, it is far easier to give money than love — but wait a minute. Not for one minute am I suggesting parents can't or won't give love. They will, but sometimes in the form of saying "no." And it's hard to know whether young people will understand that form of love.

Can parental love seem too demanding? Can a denial of rights (use of the car, curtailment of a house privilege, denial of money for a flashy pair of jeans, possibly say "love" to a child or even a teenager? Gosh, it's hard to know how they'll take it. I know the agony.

It's far easier to see the situation once all the kids have grown and flown. Sure, I can tell you how to handle all such situations, interpret what love really means to young people. Easy. It will cost me nothing now, for there are no responsibilities to shape young lives left in my stable.

Only one thing I know for sure—and I share it with you—take it or leave it. The most important thing in the lives of a babe or a brash, unruly teenager is a vast amount of love, not money or 'things' or great clothes or food. Just love and a sense of security in that love. A house is only a building. A home is where people gather who have a common bond and share bad days along with good ones, even when the good days are scarce. A home filled with concern and caring is a rich place to be. But yes, without question, that eminent writer, Tennessee Williams, spoke a genuine truth. It's easier to give money than love. Tsk.

It's a major undertaking, this parenting kids. I'll leave you to either seethe over my comments, or, hopefully, nod your head in approval because the things I have written mesh with your ideas. Sincerely hope we are on the same wave length!

DUMP PICKING
A LOST ART

That wife of mine is never satisfied with a
thing I make. She is only satisfied if I make two.
—B. Perry, 1957

 GUESS I AM ABOUT AS concerned for the environment and what we will do with our garbage as the next person, but I have to tell you right now, I miss the opportunity to go dump picking! My husband used to take the monthly load of trash off on a morning and more often than not come home with as much as he left. He was pretty discriminating too. Of course, Bernie could take a broken chair or a table top down to the cellar, spend a few hours gluing and scraping and fix the piece almost as good as new. He was pretty ingenious that way. But, I'm convinced, dump-picking was a way of life for a lot more people than Bernie.

If you ask around, betcha' you'd find people who spent a lot of time at their local dump looking over things left by others. Think about bottles. Farm houses in another era had their own plot for castoffs, if in fact, they ever threw anything away. At one time I lived in a place where treasures from another era were unearthed when a cellar was being dug.

Wondrous bottles, pale blue or soft green were unearthed. Many broken, of course, but a surprising number still intact. In my kitchen window there is a forest green (a most unusual color for glass) bottle that catches the sun in a marvelous way. I found that and many others. Some I sold (bottle collectors still roam the world); others were given to friends who oohed and ahhed over them.

One hunting season Bernie and several men friends went Down East to hunt. He seldom went to that part of the state but his instinct was working. He came home with a treasure. I remember the conversation when he arrived home.

"Did you get a deer?"

"No, but I got something else. You can go out and look, it's in the back of the pick-up. If you don't want it, I'll just break it up for firewood." He surely knew me better than that!

"What is it?" I asked, all curious.

"You just go out and see for yourself."

Nothing else was discussed before I rushed out to the barn to see what he had acquired. What I found was a cupboard—well, more like the bottom of cupboard—with a sink in the top. It was, to my genuine surprise, an authentic dry sink—something I had been coaxing him to make for me.

"Oh, Bernie," I said, "It's great. Where did you get it?"

"We stumbled onto an old fallen down farm way back in the woods. I saw this and knew it was something you'd been asking for. It's pretty rough now, but I think when I get all the paint off, it will look pretty good. Lots of the molding was off it, but I scrounged all around the area and think I located most of the pieces, although some are broken. Guess I can reconstruct somehow. Like it?"

Did I ever! Not only was it exactly what I had seen in a colonial home magazine, but the fact that he had thought about his kinda' demanding wife back home while he was off on his own, was just as impressive to me.

It took a couple of months at the workbench to scrape all the paint away, repair the hinge on the door and secure the delicate molding around the panels on the sides. When it was finished, he waxed the rich, clear wood to a fine patina and brought it up the stairs to me.

"Where are you going to put this thing?" he asked very unceremoniously. Far be it from him to let me believe he thought much of it as a piece of furniture for our home. He really did, you know, but that's how men act sometimes.

It was stunning, a real conversation piece. For more than ten years, it held a place of honor in our living room acting as a repository for plants, books, and bric-a-brac.

One day when we were very low on money for a college-bound son, an antique dealer came by. The price she offered was amazing and we felt we could not pass it up. It left the house but there have been many times I regretted the speedy transaction. I just hope it is gracing some other lady's home as lovingly as it did ours. I treasure the memory that it was *my* husband who saw its potential, sacked it home to me, and gave it a new beauty. That memory is mine forever.

A 1990 VALENTINE STORY

*Marriage is a thing you've
got to give your whole mind to.*
—Henrik Ibsen, 1869
The League of Youth

AKE AND LORRAINE BAKER often leave the paid staff to handle the noon trade at Boynton's Market in Hallowell. That seems the only time they can be together in their busy day, so they go out to lunch.

Life for this down-to-earth couple has always been a study in togetherness. They courted all through high school. Jake was a star athlete and Lorraine dutifully attended every game and waited outside the locker room to be walked home after the evening's event. Being apart for the few months she was away at college proved to be too hard to take, so she came home and married Jake.

All that was nearly four decades and five children ago, yet the sparkle has never left their relationship. Today they share the chores in keeping their business thriving. Jake opens up at 5 a.m., but has been at the store for an hour sweeping, arranging shelves, putting on the coffee pot and doughnuts. He is the fixture early birds chat with as they sip morning brew and pick up the daily paper.

If it's her day to take an early shift, Lorraine arrives about nine to tend the front cash register, leaving Jake to take care of the meat counter—a task that has earned him a modest reputation for the cuts he puts in his meat cooler.

This store business is their latest venture and after ten years, they feel they have been pretty successful.

Now you might think something like 24 hours of each other's company over the years would have left Jake, if not Lorraine, taking things for granted. You might think the romance in their marriage has faded and that they know each other so well there is no longer any mystique in their lives.

Not so.

It was just two days after Valentine's Day last year that I stopped by to do my weekly shopping. Lorraine was alone at the front of the store and we had a moment to exchange comments about local doings. When she passed me my bundles, Lorraine pointed to her finger and said,

"I waited 39 years for this, and it was well worth the wait." On her ring finger was a stunning one carat diamond, set in white gold and surrounded by 16 smaller stones. A stunning estate ring.

"Jake always said he would get me a diamond some day, but I never thought I would have such a beautiful one. He went and picked it out all by himself—I couldn't have found anything I liked better. I still can't believe it—nor can I take my eyes off it," she said.

"Was it an anniversary gift?"

"No, we planned to have dinner together on Valentine's Day, so as soon as we left the store we went down the street to Slate's Restaurant and had a great meal. During dessert, the waitress brought in a small plate on which was a white napkin folded in the form of a flower. Right in the middle of the flower I spotted something shiny and asked Jake if they were doing something special for the special day. He said he supposed so, but why didn't I pull the petals of the napkin apart and see what was there. When I did, I saw this gorgeous ring. I can tell you, I nearly fainted!"

"Your husband is a real romantic, isn't he?" I asked.

"He really is. We have weathered a lot of storms, but now that we have the kids grown and out on their own, we are picking up right where we were when we were courting during high school. You might say, we are in our second teenagehood, and loving every day of it."

Until recently, the family jewels that Lorraine referred to were the five sons the couple sired. No longer. There is a more precise meaning when she makes the reference now. A diamond ring——one she was promised years ago and one her man never forgot to give her.

RAILROAD MEMORIES

*Objects which are usually the motives of our
travels by land and by sea are often overlooked
and neglected if they lie under our eye...*
—Pliny the Elder,
Letters

T HERE'S MORE THAN A LITTLE drama waiting for the train to arrive or depart at the railroad station. It's a part of life that, unfortunately, today's youngsters never experience. This thought came to mind the other day as I read a story written in 1925. The story recounted the thrill of seeing the bright headlight of the steaming engine rounding the bend in the roadway south of the depot. The short piece was all I needed to send me into a reverie of times I stood on the wooden platform beside the tracks where the iron horse would arrive.

Waiting for the train in Millinocket was apt to be a frigid experience if the wait took place during the winter. The wind that blew directly off Mount Katahdin was enough to challenge even the hardiest. There were many Friday evenings we waited for old #7 to chug into view, muffled up to the eyes as we leaned into the breeze. It was a short time between train arrival and bundling ourselves into the old Model A to head for town with our visitor in tow.

There were some good things about waiting in the cold. Almost always other families were there waiting to gather visitors, too. It was a social event for all of us.

Then there was the Bangor Station with all the excitement of a big city, you know. We were often there for basketball tournaments; most of the games in Northern Maine were played in that city. There is, however, a far more important recollection. That was on August 19, 1944.

The infamous Greeting to my husband-of-only-two-months had been received on July 19, and it was the beginning of a two and a half year separation. Not the happiest of times, you can be sure.

I was not alone; there were dozens of wives, sweethearts and mothers at the station that day. Life was uncertain. Would they come home again after basic training? Would they be shipped directly to some foreign land? Would we see each other again in a few months—or, Heaven forbid, not for years?

I diligently tried to keep that stiff upper lip, but knew at the last minute I would break down. I did, of course. But then I wasn't the only one—there were lots of tears shed that day and hundreds of other days at railroad stations across the land when loved ones left for parts unknown. One positive thing about such a leave taking—there was a kind of camaraderie. We shared the pathos and in some strange way supported each other. Railroads did that for you. You were part of a crowd and no matter the occasion, you blended into it in a way that was rather comforting.

Over the next two years I got a lot of experience waiting for trains, getting on them and getting off them. So often, in fact, that I never see a war-time train pulling into a station during a movie that I don't get a lump in my throat. The memory of all that part of life is just too vivid.

Strange thing about dates. It was a cold January 19 in 1946 that my friend Gerry and I took the train from Millinocket to meet our men just back from the sweltering heat of the South Pacific. The long awaited telegram had arrived a week earlier announcing they had docked in San Diego and would call the minute they had word they were free to travel East. That was a frustrating week. If you've ever waited for such an important telephone call, you know what I mean.

You know the train was late! It would just have to be. We walked the platform, went inside and drank coffee, called the hotel to be sure our hotel reservations would be saved, back to the platform and yet more waiting. It was more than two hours after the expected time of arrival that we heard the whistle and caught sight of that wondrous light shining through the winter sky.

The emotions, as I remember them, were too complex to explain. Anxiety—had I changed—even more important, had he changed? Would he still be glad I was his wife after all he had seen and gone through? The initial greeting was scaring me more than I wanted to admit. Decisions, big decisions, had to be made. Where would we live? What would he find for work?

Amazingly, as soon as I saw him, my worries melted into nothing. He looked the same and as he came rushing toward me, I knew he was home and that all was right in our world. Portland station, that night, might have been the Taj Mahal or Buckingham Palace for all I knew. My husband was in my arms and nothing else in the world mattered.

Yep, railroad stations, if it has been your good fortune

to know them, carry lots of memories. Not for a minute would I want to relive even the good ones, but I like to think back to the way of life they were part of. If there's a wish in this whole piece, it is that we might once again be able to walk down to the station, buy our ticket and wait for the conductor to step down from the parlor car and shout out "ALLL ABOOOAAARD!"

MY LIFE AS A WORM PICKER

I cannot but think that he who finds a certain proportion of pain and evil inseparably woven up in the life of the very worms, will bear his own share with more courage and submission.
—Thomas Henry Huxley, 1854
On the Educational Value of the Natural History Sciences

I T WAS YEARS AGO when Charlie Strong stopped by the house late one afternoon and wanted a word or two with my sons. It seemed that Charlie had a smart little bait business going at his lake-side home. The demand was greater than his supply so he was looking for sturdy-backed lads to swell his night crawler inventory.

My sons, after listening politely, seemed pretty lukewarm to me. Convinced that if they stayed up half the night catching night crawlers, they would be too exhausted the next day to wrestle, argue, and act the typical boys, I pointed out how welcome the jangle of change in their pockets would sound! Further, I stressed physical fitness (I lived to find this a complete misconception). Grudgingly, the boys agreed that if Charlie would come back the last of the week they would have some night crawlers for him.

Obviously the first thing needed was a flashlight. Nothing we owned that was supposed to throw lights did it well; most threw no light at all. There were many interesting conversations about who was and was not responsible for flashlights that did not work. After we got batteries, the light question was resolved.

Agility is also a must for the successful night crawler forage. It would seem the easiest thing in the world would be to grasp a fat worm by the midsection and quickly pop it into the can you carry as you scour the dewy grass. Ah no, quite the opposite.

After your eyes adjust to the night search, you spot your first worm. You lunge, assured that success is in your grip - but actually what you clasp is nothing more than a handful of wet lawn and if the lunge has been a vigorous one, probably a good yard of gravel.

This delicate performance is eventually perfected and you snag your first luscious night crawler. With this conquest, you start mentally counting your catch. The trick, of course, is to keep track of the number of worms, because who wants to dump them all out and pick each one over again to get the correct count? When, however, you grab at your prey so forcefully that the little thing is rendered divided, you do not add two; you subtract one!

The boys got under way and picked up a fair-sized collection of worms, but the one who truly got bit by the night crawling bug was of course the one least likely to succeed, over the long haul at least. Me!

The hardest part of my evening adventure was staying awake until it got dark enough for the little fellows to come out of hiding. Darkness comes late during the Maine summer. Once started, any sleepiness was dispelled by the cool summer evening.

Here again - there is a paradox. Warm, dry summer

evenings are not the ideal time for pursuing this kind of fish bait. What one really needs is a good steady drizzle.

And that, my friends, is what broke this camel's back. At 40-plus years, with damp, cool earth meeting slightly aging knees, you can guess what caused my downfall—arthritic complaints. The cash flow suddenly ceased for me but the lads went merrily on amassing a tidy sum that was banked at the season's end.

Looking back I find that I grew to have a fond affection for those wonderful little creatures that are such a blessing in the garden. I now treat them more kindly as I work the soil around the flower bed. I cover them carefully when they appear and leave them in peace with not a qualm for all the baitless fishermen we know.

THE CHAIR

A workman that needeth not
to be ashamed
—The Bible,
2 Timothy

ANIEL BARTLETT MCLAUGHLIN, or D.B. as the local folk called him, was a farmer and cabinet maker who sired three sons and one daughter. Born April 26, 1834, in China, Maine, D.B. early in life settled in Levant, Maine, where he met, wooed and married Rachel Tilton Boyd.

Back in the 1870's the winters were long and without much diversion, so it is assumed D.B. thought to use his long winter evenings to make a rocking chair to grace the family parlor. Sometime during the winter of 1870 the chair was started, and work on it progressed slowly but steadily over the next ten years.

D.B.'s chair would be made from the entire butt of a beech tree. After he selected and felled the tree, D.B. found the center was partly decayed, so the amount of scraping and digging out was lessened. It would have a circular shape so he set to work cutting away all the part of the tree that was not needed. The entire procedure was hand labor, the material was solid hardwood, and long hours of labor were needed. As the butt took on the appearance of a functional household furnishing, a lesser man would have counted his task complete. In D.B., however, an artisan had been born.

A design, he now decided, should be carved in the wood. Much thought surely was given to this phase of the chair. D.B.'s wife, Rachel, was consulted, because this would have to be pleasing, not only to her eye, but to the eyes of the ladies' sewing group who, she was sure, would look at D.B.'s work with envy. After long contemplation, D.B. decided that a cut-out design would be appropriate, and would be a real challenge to his ability. It is said that he drew the pattern himself and used "all kinds of tools" to cut it out.

With the completion of the design the process of smoothing all the round edges began. Hundreds of hours of tedious sanding were required to create its satin smooth texture. The body of the chair was done. For the rockers D.B. chose rock maple as the best wood for wear and workability.

Finished at last, the chair was given pride of place in a corner of the parlor of the "Old Spooner" house in Levant. There must have been many compliments for D.B.'s work.

Some four years after D.B. began his chair Rachel had thoughts on a creation of her own. On January 5, 1874, "the coldest day of the year," she presented D.B. with their third son and fourth child. Wee Cyrus Ladd, as the child was named, was the only babe of Rachel and D.B.'s brood to be rocked in that chair. In the 118 years since then, it would be hard to guess how many babies have been cuddled in it.

Albert, the second son, inherited D.B.'s chair. When fire ravaged the house in Levant, he courageously rescued it from the flames. Only one rocker was broken, and was carefully replaced.

The chair passed from Albert to Cyrus, who had been the first baby to know the rhythm of its rock. It remained his most prized possession until his death in 1967 at 93. In 1942 Cyrus married my mother, and it came to me after her death.

D.B.'s creation is today an irreplaceable antique. Certainly nowhere is there another quite like it. Being responsible for such a unique piece of furniture caused me concern and finally I approached the Maine State Museum with the intent of donating the chair to that institution if they would accept it. Once the staff saw a photograph of the chair and learned that it was factually documented, they seemed anxious to acquire it for their collection.

In May, 1988 the McLaughlins and the Perrys gave over all rights to this piece of folk art, hand crafted in Levant, Maine more than a hundred years earlier. D.B.'s rocking chair has found a permanent home. Its artistry and workmanship will be seen and appreciated by countless generations of museum visitors in the years to come.

HOW ABOUT APRIL IN...QUEBEC?

*There is hardly a bigger pleasure than
to do a good deed in secret, and
then see it discovered by chance.*
—French Proverb

F YOU CAN'T MAKE Paris in April, the next best thing is Quebec. A bright morning walk around that Canadian city is so delightful, I'll settle for it at any time of the year.

Although I have never visited Paris, I suspect Quebec is as scenic, as clean and as charming as its European counterpart. Quebec, the April morning I was there, was well swept and free of litter (with the exception of a naked wine bottle poking its head from a snowbank here and there). Spring was just arriving. Birds were flying from tree to tree and shopkeepers were bravely opening their doors to welcome the sun. The heavenly smell of croissants fresh from the oven wafted from bakeries. People were friendly and spoke or nodded a greeting as they passed.

In spite of the April sun the air was sharp. Wind blowing from the St. Lawrence River below the parade grounds was unrelenting and soon chilled my exposed ears. Fortunately I found a kerchief in my bag and wrapped it around my head. This gave protection, but surely made me look like a vagabond. No matter, that. The day was too beautiful and I was too involved with the sights and sounds of the city to care, even the slightest bit, about appearances.

It was on a small street of shops parallel to the Basilica that we saw a group of young women chatting together jubilantly. As we came nearer we saw they were stopping people along the way and selling or handing out what we thought at first were pamphlets. When they stopped us we were at a loss to know the reason. Our ignorance of the French language was utterly frustrating.

One of the group, an attractive young woman in a long blue great coat and a chic red beret, offered me a small brown paper bag folded as if it were empty. She spoke in French but when I shook my head in embarrassment, she switched to English.

"Let me give you a treasure."

"A treasure? What kind of treasure?" I asked.

"It is—how you say—a good luck thing, perhaps." Her eyes sparkled as she explained, and the warmth and sincerity of her smile won me over completely.

"Please, take the bag. Open it and read your treasure!"

I did as she said. Within the bag was a small piece of white paper with a handwritten message in French: "*Il n'y point de plus grand plaisir que de faire une bonne action en cachette et de la voir decouvrir par hasard.*"

I knew only enough words to guess at the meaning, but the precise message was beyond me.

"Will you translate for me?" I asked, "Do I pay you?"

"No pay. It is only a school project to give happiness on this pretty day. Nice? Is it not a treasure?," she asked.

Then she took the paper and as she read, I wrote on the envelope, "There is hardly a bigger pleasure than to do a good deed in secret, and then see it discovered by chance."

Our eyes met in understanding as I thanked her, for indeed she had shared a not-to-be-forgotten treasure.

Such a simple thing, but perfect in its way.

PAY DAY ROUTINE

Be silent and safe…
Silence never betrays you.
John Boyle O'Reilly
Rules of the Road

WHEN MY GRANDPARENTS moved to Maine's "Magic City" (Millinocket) at the turn of the century, they were, by anyone's standards, poor people. The burgeoning paper industry brought other poor families to the area, and provided a weekly pay check. It was anything but abundant, but then the new workers were used to far less. They were happy for the opportunity to give their families more than they had had in the past.

My grandfather Luke must have been a wise man. I knew him and his homespun philosophy far too short a time. His youngest daughter, Aunt Margaret, has told me of the pay day ritual he carried out each week.

"Pay day was the big day of the week. When Pappa got home from the mill we were all waiting for him near the porch steps. It was an impatient supper we ate that night.

"When the meal was cleared away the whole family climbed the stairs to the bedroom he and Mama shared. From high in the house's largest closet, Pappa brought out the strongbox. With a small key he kept on his watch chain, he unlocked it. There, for all to see, was enough money to sail to Spain, to buy a king's palace or feed half of Prince Edward Island, the hallowed land of his birth," Aunt Margaret said.

"With great ceremony, Pappa took the pay envelope from inside his coat pocket (Pappa always wore a suit coat). He broke the seal on the envelope and dumped bills and coins onto the bed. Carefully he assembled all the denominations on top of those accumulated in previous weeks. While we watched this activity we counted along, eyed the soiled green bills and relished the jingle of the coins. We, each of us, were impressed with the richness of our lot.," she continued.

"Once the money was sorted, it was replaced—in exquisite order—in the box, which was closed and locked. The key was put back on the chain and dropped into Pappa's vest pocket, and the box put back onto the closet shelf. The ceremony was over for another week. Our family went back downstairs secure in the knowledge that we possessed more money than we would ever be able to spend."

Investors will poohpooh the ritual. Bankers will shudder. Economists will consider it a deplorable lesson. If they do, I think they miss the point. Perhaps I read too much into this simple activity from 70 years ago, but there seems more to it than ritual.

Don't we too often deprive our children of the advantage of sharing family money, family responsibilities and hardships? Wouldn't we do well to share with them the knowledge of where the money comes from, where it goes (how many understand the fuel, electric and food bills) and that it belongs to the *family*, not just Mom and Dad?

My aunts and uncles felt secure. They had seen the

BEACH ENCOUNTER

My life is like a stroll upon the beach,
as near the ocean's edge as I can go.
—Henry David Thoreau

I T WAS A DAMP, FOGGY Sunday afternoon, as is so often the case near the ocean. In spite of the weather I was determined to take my daily stroll along the Kildare Capes in Prince Edward Island. The red beach is a temptress.

It's a long strand and the tide was receding, leaving small reefs exposed along the shore. I wandered up and down kicking an interesting stone here and there, eyeing pieces of driftwood and popping some into my plastic bag to add to a pile I was collecting for a future lobster bake.

At the end of a long walk there was a gap of water running seaward from an inland pond. Days of rain had make a sizable run of it. It was now so wide, in fact, that I felt it unwise to go further without proper footwear. I sat on a ridge of broken rock and viewed the scene. Placid, lovely, soothing.

Off to the right was a gradual ridge where trucks bring horses down to the shore to harvest Irish moss. As I looked in that direction I saw a woman meandering down toward the shore with what I took to be the family pooch at her heels.

My reverie continued but when later I looked up I saw the trailing figure was not a dog but a child. A little girl, enchanted with the surf. She ran to the edge and scurried back as it neared her spot. The woman was relaxed and allowed the child to explore and adventure.

I watched as they came closer, then stopped, as I had done, near the gap in the beach. The child tossed pebbles into the rushing water and shrieked with delight as they flowed away. She eased nearer and nearer the water, but came back dry from each encounter. Her laughter, shouts of joy and clapping hands were infectious and I was caught up in her excitement. We waved to each other. The wind and surf and plummeting water made talking impossible.

The child, a three-year-old, I guessed, had been carrying a small red object in her hand. Finally that too was tossed into the onrushing stream. Child and adult followed its descent, hoping at each spot to intercept its voyage to the sea. From my perch I reasoned that the surf might catch the red toy and hurl it back toward shore on my side of the gap. I ran toward the beach and waited. Sure enough, it came nearly to my feet. I waited to reach for it until the water receded, then picked it up.

The child was beside herself with delight. She jumped up and down, clapping and shouting. It was half a cork float— nothing valuable, unless, that is, you happen to be a three-year-old experiencing the way of water and toys for the first time.

I walked to where the pair stood on the opposite side of the gap and with a poor toss winged it to them. The child picked it up and, jumping with excitement, once again threw it into the stream. Again I followed it to the shore and again acted as her retriever and tossed it over. It was a game—a delightful game for both of us.

Gradually our late June afternoon adventure slowed down and, still without a word, our paths took different directions. With a wave, the ladies turned to the ridge behind them and I began my walk home.

A simple thing, this, surely. But is it not the simple things that make life enjoyable? The child's wonderful sense of happiness was a treasure to witness. The woman's willingness to let the little girl set her own limits with the surf, and my luxury in being part of this afternoon's frolic will stay with me for a long time. I hope the little lady will remember our afternoon on the beach too.

CLIPPING MADNESS?

Every life is many days, day after day we walk
through ourselves meeting Robbers, Ghosts, Old men,
Young men, Wives, Widows, Brothers-in-Love.
But always meeting ourselves.
—James Joyce
Ulysses

A FEW YEARS AGO I took a three-day cruise along the Maine coast in a windjammer. One of the most delightful people on the trip was Nannette Pope. I had originally met Nannette at an Elderhostel and we had immediately connected. Nannette had recently moved to Massachusetts after a lengthy stint with the U.S. Department of Labor in Washington. Before that she had been a columnist with the *Chicago Tribune*, and this may have contributed to our mutual attraction. Nannette was spending her retirement days doing family research and we made plans to travel to Ireland together so she could continue her diggings.

I called her one evening not too long after the windjammer cruise ended. No answer. Some weeks later I tried again and after several rings a very weak voice answered. She was recovering from emergency surgery, but was doing very well and planned to be out and about in a few weeks. I promised to call her the following week, just to check up.

When I did, again no one answered. My immediate thought was she had really improved and was out for the evening. I tried several days later. No answer.

It was about three weeks from the last call that I got a letter from Nannette's son, Robert Polk. His mother had not survived her convalescence. She was being interred the day I had called her.

Why do I tell you this? Well, there are a couple of reasons. First, the obvious, is how fleeting life is! In the snap of a finger it could be over for any of us. But on a more cheerful note, I wonder how many children would be thoughtful enough to make the gesture Robert did in writing me. After all, his mother and I were hardly long-time friends. We had met only months before. Somehow he knew I was concerned for her and would want to know. I was then, and am still, grateful for his consideration.

One thing I will always remember about this spunky Irish lady was that she was a "clipper." Every time she wrote she included a clipping from something she had read that she felt would interest me.

"All writers are clippers, Katy," she told me, with a twinkle in her eye. "We are forever sharing our thoughts and interests with people we hope will feel the same way we do. Some do and some don't, but we keep on clipping."

My Aunt Margie is also a clipper. Her contributions are more often an account of a play she's attended or what the weather is like in L.A. I suspect Margie lets the paper tell me what she has done and spares herself the recounting.

Sue Mahoney is a stunning young lady that I grew to be very fond of while we were in Belize together. This affection resulted in part because her father back in the States cut out all the *Far Side* cartoons and sent them off to her each week. Sue shared them first with Jon Briggs and Jon, in turn, passed them along to me. The three of us chuckled over each of them when we met at the Peace Corps office. Nothing like a good laugh to cement friendship.

I find myself falling into the same habit. It's getting so I read the paper with the scissors at hand. Almost daily I see something that reminds me of a particular person. Most times I reconsider before sending the item off, but it's a fact, I am bent on sharing what I read with others. Lately I've been sending some comic strips along to grandchildren who I feel will connect with the humor.

Do you suppose it is also a sign of aging when one wants to share a feeling, a laugh, or simply a non-important thought with another person? That just might be the answer.

CHRIS

AN EXTRAORDINARY HUMAN BEING

*"You gals, quick, get a big rock—
chuck the back wheels!"*
—Chris
"We are ready! Let the balloon fly."
—Christina and Karl Olson,
letter to friends

T HE BEST DECISION I made in 1982 was to join Chris and Karl Olson for a two-week cart trip through the Peloponnisos peninsula in Greece. Today I am doubly glad I went on that Grassroots Educational Expedition. The opportunity to share such an experience no longer exists. Last month Chris died in a North Carolina hospital as the result of a cerebral hemorrhage.

Chris Olson might have been a Gypsy, a Greek, an Italian, or a Spaniard. Her swarthy complexion, bright dark eyes and long auburn hair, which she wore curled into a neat bun when the weather was warm or hanging loose but carefully contained when it was cool, was indeed a face that any nationality would be proud to claim. The most infectious part of her classic face, however, was her ever-present smile. A smile that made it impossible for anyone in her company not to respond in kind.

After receiving the tragic news of her death last week, some incident of our brief association flashed through my mind almost hourly. A song she sang, a joke she spun, the way she cuddled her adopted Haitian son, Jeremy, even her body movements, as efficient and directed as an arrow. Little wonder it's hard to forget.

The way Chris handled young people was simple and direct. One of our group was a 12-year-old. The hours we spent learning a few Greek phrases did not excite her. Sensing her indifference, Chris said, without any hostility at all, "Hey, if you don't want to learn Greek, no problem. You'll only need it for two weeks here. Forget it, if you'd rather."

Nothing more. No pressure. But there was a turn-around. The youngster began to try harder, perhaps to prove to Chris that she cared. Chris had a way of letting kids make their own decisions, but she insisted they live with those decisions once made.

Authority. That was something easy to note in her personality. As the horses strained to pull the loaded carts up a hill, Chris took command.

"We'll have to rest the horses often. Dorothy, you and Betty pick up a good-sized rock and be ready to 'chuck" the back wheels when we stop. The rest of you keep up with us and be ready to spell them."

Some of us were having quite a time keeping up—the elevation was impressive—but keep up we did. Who would *dare* not follow her orders!

When the brightly painted carts rolled into a Greek village, we watched doors open and folks come out, waving and calling to others to come see. The Olsons had traveled the area for ten years or more and their caravans were well known, perhaps as those of the "crazy Americans!" The villagers' interest and excitement seemed genuine. This entourage may have been the only thing they knew of our country. Chris and Karl may, quite unwittingly, have forged a valuable link between the two lands.

Greek mornings were cool and the Olsons were out of bed and busy early. Gathering wood for the fire and putting water on for coffee was a ritual they liked to do before the rest of us got up. When breakfast making got under way, Chris held court over a gigantic fry pan heated by the smallest fire you can imagine. Into the warmed pan she poured a generous splash of olive oil which fried thick slabs of Greek bread, or pancakes or scrambled eggs laced with a hard, Greek cheese. Whatever the menu, amazing things happened when she hunkered near the ground to cook. She had that knack.

One evening we camped a short distance from Mycenae. As we sat in the fire glow, Chris began telling the story of Agamemnon and Clytemnestra, in words that Homer would never have believed.

"See, this dude, who is not your cool kind of guy at all, takes a knife and cuts off his son's head. Now you gotta admit that was some tacky stunt to pull. No wonder his wife didn't look forward to his coming home nights!"

She went into details of the myth in such descriptive language that kids and oldsters alike would remember the story forever. But, you see, Chris was not hard up for more traditional language. When she offered grace before meals, her words were rich and beautiful and fraught with conviction.

Then there was a long walk down into a cistern, far below ground, just beyond the ancient walls of Mycenae. We each took a taper from Chris, lighted it, and began the 100-step descent. Soon the light from the opening above was gone and we began feeling our way carefully one step at a time, down, down, down, until we came to a large pool of water. Chris suggested we sit down and listen. Quiet descended upon us. The candlelight danced on the overhead rock and we breathed as one. Then Chris began to sing. Hymns, rounds, camp tunes we had all learned years ago. It was a hauntingly beautiful sound. Resonant melodies with a suggestion of harmony echoed up the stairs and back to us. We joined in, but before long I could sing no more. My eyes were full of tears and my throat was tight. It was a spiritual experience unlike any other in my life.

When the time came to fly back home I found I had bought far more than I could handle. A backpack, a duffle bag, two Greek blankets, a *flocati* (rug), and a stuffed suitcase. Too much! The other nine travelers had been equally unwise in their purchases. Chris came to the rescue.

"Okay, Katy, I'll be with you after I see what I can do for Ceil," she answered when I said I must leave something behind.

She looked at the pile and then began stuffing. The sleeping bag, blankets, *flocati* and other things went into the duffle and before long everything was condensed into three heavy but manageable packs. She went up and down the corridors of the Hotel Orion in Athens bringing order out of purchased chaos.

Chris Olson was a superb actress, a gentle nurse, a jovial companion and friend, an exceptional organizer, and a lady who never spared herself but gave freely of her love and compassion. In everything she did her devoted life partner stood back and glowed in her light. Karl was a perfect complement and a necessary ingredient in her life. Without him Chris could never have been Chris. They were, if such is possible, a perfect blend of personalities.

In her brief three-plus decades, hundreds of people from all walks of life rubbed elbows, as I did, with Chris Olson. I wonder if they were as impressed as I? I often thought she did everything right, but of course that's not true. She was a very human, human being and knew her share of frustration, anger and hostility, but it just didn't seem as though she knew as much of these things as the rest of us.

Chris taught me things I will never forget. For these lessons and for being Chris—in two short weeks, I learned to love her.

Requiscat in pacem, dear Chris.

CLOTHESLINES
A BEACON OF HOME

Nothing grows in our garden, only washing.
And babies.

                —Dylan Thomas

OR MORE THAN 65 years I have been fascinated with clothes hanging out to dry. Perhaps it began in 1925, when I first watched my mother carry a wicker basket of wet family laundry up the cellar stairs balanced on her right hip, a bunch of wooden pins jiggling on top of the pile. The day comes back as clearly as yesterday because that was the morning a postal card arrived stating my darling Uncle Eddie would be coming home from his trip to Canada in a day or two.

On that long ago day I watched Mom, pins easily accessible in her mouth, hang one garment after another on the rope line beside the house, each one beginning to waft and wave in the spring sunshine.

My interest in clotheslines was heightened, years later, by a charming book showing clotheslines around the United States. It was clear the family clothesline could portray the life of a family.

Unfortunately, this visual symbol of a common household chore hardly exists today. The days when we judged the weather before we began the Monday laundry are gone. Weather is not a factor when we remain in our warm kitchens or washrooms to pop a load into the washing machine, transfer the cleaned items into the nearby dryer, close the door and read a book during the drying process. Folding and returning the clothes or linen to the appropriate place never necessitates a step out of the house. Smelling of flower-scented "softener" or soaps, the laundry is pleasant, but there's an artificiality about the process.

Give me, if you will, a towel or blouse that has whipped in a March breeze during the lengthening days of spring. The weather outside has filled the towels and sheets with sun, wind, maybe even a shower, and the smell is ambrosia. Towel yourself after such drying and your senses savor the freshness and clean smell of springtime and life.

Laundry whipping on the line does signify life, it seems to me. A pair of men's work pants dancing next to a dangling cotton shirt sends a message of people. Dish towels and bedding meld nicely with other household pieces, and say something of the people who use these articles.

My interest in clotheslines has followed me to all parts of the world. It was on a spring morning that we drove up a long, twisting drive to an Irish castle. We had spotted the structure miles before we reached the driveway, and it so resembled the opening scene of a Disney show I wanted to see it closer. We were bold to attempt such an intrusion in a foreign land.

From the top of the drive the view was astounding. The castle was perched on a promontory of land that jutted into the Atlantic Ocean. Grazing sheep dotted long green fields sweeping down to a high cliff.

We drove our small English car slowly past the land-scape and around to the back of the large stone building. Behold—just off the back step, a pair of linen tea towels jumped in the breeze. It was a beckoning, friendly and familiar. Those pieces of native cloth were motivation enough to give us courage.

We knocked at the door and were answered by a smiling Irishman who greeted us as if we were family. Our boldness resulted in a tour of the magnificent holiday home of the late Lord Mountbatten—all because of tea towels drying in a bright Irish sun.

Then there were the clotheslines strung under high-posted Belize homes. Mothers were up early and at their morning stint with the scrub board. The women living in those homes turned out the most beautiful laundry I have ever seen. It was as if neighbor vied with neighbor to string the cleanest, brightest laundry on the street, laundry that would cause Procter & Gamble to hide their corporate eyes in envy. Throughout the day, in rain or shine, the Belizean wash was a sight to behold. My appreciation for the results of the early morning wash was heightened by the knowledge that I wasn't expected to go back home to a similar task.

I'm not going so far as to suggest that clotheslines should come back in vogue, but that might not be such a bad idea. There's a certain sense of accomplishment in toting a basket of wet clothes to the back yard. It does get you out of doors, where you might just see spring leaves unfurling in a nearby maple tree, or hear the song of a returning bird.

Homemakers know the secret of taking pleasures, big or little, where we find them.

OLD RED

*Nature binds truth, happiness and virtue
together as by an indissoluble chain.*
—Marquis De Condorcet,
Sketches for a Historical Picture

NCLE FRED LOVED the woods. Many years ago he and his wife Ruth had found a plot of land near a small pond and built a camp. Every month of the year Fred came to this remote Maine place and spent days doing what he liked best. He fished, watched the birds and animals, read books and listened to music. He never wore a watch or cared a bit about the time of day. He ate when he was hungry and slept when he was tired. Time was something he spent as he felt the need.

What pleased Fred more than anything was becoming as much like the animals he befriended as he could.

"Animals are a lot smarter than man," he often said, "They live according to their needs and don't give a hoot who has the most money or the most power. They are satisfied to have food—and are not above fighting to get it, ya' know— a place to sleep, an animal of the opposite sex to breed with, that's all they want, Some people think they are complicated. They are not!" On this point, Fred is insistent.

If Ol' Red and Uncle Fred became a twosome, it's not surprising. "About ten years ago I went up to open Camp One Eye in the spring. It was a year with lotsa' snow and the spring runoff was a torrent." Fred sat at the dining room table sipping tea as he recounted the story.

"I had quite a time packing the canoe with grub enough to spend a week or two away. Pretty tricky thing, ya' know, stowin' things just right to balance the load, with me in the rear to be considered. Well, sir, finally I got it all aboard and set off for camp. It's a long paddle the five miles from where I leave the car to camp, and the wind was *not* at my back as I wished it had been."

Fred is no stranger to the long haul and made good time, pulling away, and nearing camp with every pull. Watching for rocks obscured by rushing water, he didn't notice the gush of water cascading from a small brook. The stream caught him amidships and threw him off balance. Before he knew it, he was in frigid water with the canoe and its contents nearly on top of him. In a split second he began doing what had to be done. He fumbled about for a length of rope, tied it to the thorps, and righted the heavily laden canoe.

"Damn good thing I had clung near the shore," Fred said. "That water was jeasley cold and all my clothes were heavier than hell. As soon as I got that canoe righted— and I was damn glad to see that I had stuffed that boat so tight nothing was lost— I waded to shore, tied up that son-of-a -bitch, and started the long, cold walk to Camp One Eye."

Fred knows the terrain like a nail on his finger. Carrying his ax and a waterproof flashlight, he hoisted his backpack onto his shoulders and took off. The exertion soon warmed him up, and within a couple of hours he had hacked his way through underbrush and finally reached open land. It was a happy sight when he reached his haven through the brush in back of the camp, a different approach than his usual one from the water.

In what seemed like less time than it takes to tell, Fred unlocked the camp, found dry wood in the shelter he had built years before, made shavings from the cedar by whittling with his jackknife, and lighted a fire. He untied his boots and, throwing off the wet clothes on his back, found dry trousers and a wool shirt from his camp wardrobe.

The event had used up all his energy and more besides. After he brewed a pot of tea and had a couple of stale crackers and peanut butter, he cozied into the bed beside the comfortable stove and waited for another day to make decisions about a rescue of goods and canoe.

Walking back to the canoe was far easier the next day in dry clothes and sunny weather. He found the canoe as he had left it, high and dry, and although he discovered a badly damaged hull would make it impossible to paddle back, the food, except for some bread and hamburg, was dry and usable.

"I decided that water-soaked bread and meat were not important enough to save, so I left it opened on a rock beside the boat. Then I hoisted as much of the gear as I could handle onto my shoulders and left. I had a good week's work ahead, coming back several times for more of the stuff, and finally getting the boat back where I had things to repair it" Fred said.

The next trip back, a day or two later, was the beginning of the Ol' Red saga.

"Half that meat was gone, cleaned up as neat as anything, but there was a little left. Right there I reasoned it must be a fox that took it. Had it been a bear, it would have cleaned up the whole thing. Well, sir, a few days later I saw this handsome red fox skulking near the camp. Somehow that fox—ya' know they call them 'sly', well, I call them 'smart'— had obviously associated that food with me and this camp. Doncha' call that smart? I do." Fred chuckled.

That proved to be the beginning of a unique friendship, one that has lasted a decade and has introduced other members of the fox family to Fred and Ruth. In fact, the relationship developed to the point where Ol' Red would eat from their hands. In summer or even winter the wily animal would be seen nestling near a tree listening to what was going on about him.

"Lotsa' times I've looked out on a winter evening, sometimes 20 below zero," Fred said, "and there was Ol' Red hunkered down listening to the radio. Fox like classical music, did you know that? That's the only kind that plays on my radio, and that old guy was lapping it up."

A few months ago Fred and Ruth returned to Camp One Eye for the first time this year. Ruth was busy setting things to rights in the camp, and Fred toured the outer terrain seeing how the land and buildings had weathered a fiercely cold winter. He had been out a sort time when Ruth heard him stomping onto the doorstep.

"Ruth, there's a maternity ward under the camp. Looks like Molly has given us a new foursome," Fred told her.

"How do you know it's Molly who presented us with this litter?" she questioned.

"Don't know, but she's about the only one I know that would be comfortable this close to us heathen humans," Fred responded. With that he went back out to further appraise the situation.

Fred is not a scientist, just an ordinary man who has an unordinary concept of life in the wild. He cares greatly about woods critters, as he terms them, and believes that those critters should be left to themselves. He insists he's more content with the wildlife than he often is with homo sapiens. It shows. This weathered codger, and he would grin at this description, is ruggedly individual. He marches to his own drummer and doesn't care a damn what others think of him. In this lies his contentment with the hand dealt him.

Fred finds nothing strange in the fact that, as far as he can determine, Molly, who was fathered by Ol' Red, became pregnant by him, and, although Ol' Red hasn't been sighted for some time, has assumed the task of keeping Fred and Ruth surrounded by a new fox family.

"You know, Molly has to be Ol' Red's daughter. She has most of his distinctive mannerisms. She cocks her head the same as he does. She curls up and lies in the same posture— and more surprising, in Ol' Red's place. In fact, until she proved she was a *she* and not Ol' Red, we weren't sure it wasn't the old feller himself. I like to think that family of foxes will be here at this campsite as long as it exists. Ruth and I'll be gone one day, but the foxes will be here. I guess I like the idea of them taking over where we leave off."

With that burst of sentiment, Fred picks up his battered old Stetson hat, wipes a wooly shirt sleeve across his mouth, and begins to take his leave.

"Ruth and I are leaving for camp in a week or two and would take a lot of pleasure having you come along, that is, if you can tolerate black flies. They're damn cussed this year, but I tell you, they are a sight easier to take than some of these jeasley speechifying politicians we gotta put up with this season. Lots easier. Think about it. We got good grub, plenty to read, lots of wildlife to enjoy, and great music. Can't beat this agenda for a retired son-of-a-bitch, can ya'?"

It will be a long day before a better offer comes my way.

EVERY MAN
LEAVES HIS MARK

You give but little when you give of your possessions.
It is when you give of yourself that you truly give.
—Kahlil Gibran

ANY YEARS AGO my husband and I decided to restore an old farmhouse. There were beautiful, wide, pine floorboards throughout the house, every one with coat upon coat of objectionable paint. I hoped we could bring these floors back to their natural beauty, but was having no luck convincing my husband that the floors were worth the considerable effort.

One morning after breakfast my stepfather, whom we called Gramp, took a small hand scraper and went up the front stairs. After a long time I went to check on his whereabouts. He was hard at work on his hands and knees in the farthest corner of a large bedroom, scraping the floor—by hand.

After seeing the beauty of that one floor, my husband agreed to do all the others as well, with an electric sander. The work was easier and faster this way, but none had the mellow rich tone of the hand-scraped bedroom floor. Gramp had put enough of himself into the work that it showed through.

In the same way, he set to work scraping a spool bed

that I hadn't been able to resist at an auction. Time was never a consideration with Gramp. After weeks of work the bed was ready to be set up, and it was beautiful.

Whenever Gramp came to visit, he always asked for the most menial jobs. He peeled apples all day for pies and apple sauce, shelled peas all season, snapped beans. He even drew the paring and chopping detail during pickle season.

Gramp never had a trade except carpentry, and this he learned from his father. His joy was in building miniatures. He was willing to put as much work and talent into a small piece as he did in the life-size objects. A friend hired him to build a fieldstone well with a roof for her garden. When the real thing was finished, Gramp decided to copy it in miniature, correct in every detail. The small well even boasted a minute hand-whittled bucket that hung on a fine, copper wire bail.

There are many people who never appear in any newspaper and who are unknown except to their family and friends, but who have made the world a little better by having passed through it. Such a man completed his ninety-three year journey through life in 1967.

His name was Cyrus Ladd McLaughlin. During the twenty-some years I knew him, nothing about him in any way set him apart or above his fellow man, except his long life and his keen awareness of all worldly events. Until two weeks before he had done with the things of this earth, he consumed one cowboy book after another, kept abreast of all political activity in his town, the state and the nation—and never once admitted that any team other than the Boston Red Sox could win the Pennant.

Consistency was never a characteristic Gramp worked to perfect, it was simply his way of life. For him there was only one political party worth mentioning, the Democratic Party.

When dinner was done and the family sat around digesting, Gramp took this as his cue to tell a story. We heard the same ones repeated, but each session produced a new one.

One story was told by him more times than I could count. He consistently refused butter or milk. As a child he had been told to drink his milk; his mother insisted. Finally, he drank it, but vowed he never would again. I think he kept that vow. And yet, I'm sure he didn't dislike these two foods, for there was never any comment or refusal when I served vegetables laced with butter.

We were amazed how he kept his stories tucked away until just the right time to tell them. Perhaps I was so engrossed with the twinkle in his eye that, no matter how often I heard a story, I couldn't repeat it exactly. So all I can say is that one of his stories went something like this:

"One of the Keith boys wasn't too bright," he would say. "When we asked him who had taken the stage into town with him, his answer was, 'I was one, the two Larrabee boys was two, Sam Plourde was three...hmm...(how was that, Joe?) Well, there was four of us, anyhow!' "

Not hilarious, but when Gramp told it we were attentive, and it always got a chuckle out of us. Sometimes we asked him to tell it just because he enjoyed the telling so much.

You see there was really nothing great or even unusual about Cy McLaughlin. He never made a name for himself but, by the same measure, he never did anyone a wrong, knowingly. That's not a bad record, after dealing with the world and all kinds of people for the major part of a century.

BARGAINS

How to live well on nothing a year
—William Makepeace Thackeray

WHO DOESN'T LOVE A bargain? You don't have to be a frugal Yankee to look for one, but perhaps those who grew up in this sparse, often inhospitable clime are more persistent in the search than others. Over the years that innate urge to use every scrid of anything available, or to make something out of nothing, or to seek the silk among the silage, has served me well. I boast, yes I do, about some treasures I have saved from destruction.

There is a lovely ironstone bowl that has graced a living room table in my home for nearly 50 years. At one time it was part of a bowl and pitcher set that provided the toilette facility that today's lavatory does. The pitcher, sorrowfully, no longer exists, but the bowl, with a circle of soft, blue flowers enhancing it, lends itself beautifully to an informal decor. Its acquisition reveals what an inquisitive eye can uncover.

It happened, during the days I was a young wife with one small child and another soon to arrive, that I needed furnishings for a large farmhouse we had just bought. Beds, tables, chairs and a few dishes were necessities—no time or money for fancy decorative appointments. But that eagle eye was alert. I was invited to accompany a neighbor who had been appointed administrator of the estate left by an aging Irish gentleman who had left no kin. I was delighted at the invitation because I had often hankered (yes, hankered is the word) to see the inside of the dilapidated old Cape.

John, the appraiser/administrator, and I went from cellar to barn, first floor to second floor, and finally opened a smoke-covered overhead door into the attic. It was a sorrowful sight, and a wonder the lovely old house had not burned or fallen in with neglect. We turned over papers brown from age and the smoke that had filtered through cracks in the floorboards. The loosely-mortared chimney was almost blocked with creosote. John and I both clucked at the neglect and the obvious need for repairs if the place were to be made habitable again.

We were ready to climb down the ladder to the second floor when I spotted a container of some sort at the back of the chimney.

"John, wait a minute," I said. I picked up the piece and, taking a tissue out of my pocket, wiped away a bit of the accumulation of years of dust and grime. What I saw was white pottery with a lovely swirl of blue decoration. "Why do you suppose this is here, John?" I asked.

"Jim may have put it here to catch some of the creosote. If he hadn't, it probably would have run right down into his bedroom and covered him before he knew it," John chuckled.

We finally determined that was probably the reason. But I had already been seized by an overwhelming desire to take it home, wash it, and get a better look at it.

"John, will this be put in the auction, do you think?"

"Are you kidding? Who would ever bid on the likes of that?" scoffed John.

"Well, I would for one. Can I buy it if it won't be for sale publicly?"

"No, you can't buy it. If you want it, take it. It will probably go to the dump when the auctioneer comes in to clean up this mess. Take it home with you. I think Jim would be pleased that some woman found things here worth wanting. He had little contact with women. His mother has been gone 30 years and he never married. Yep, Katy, I think it would please him that you'll take that old bowl home and give it a good home."

John got no argument from me. I carefully descended the ladder after passing the treasure to his upstretched hands. Into the kitchen sink full of soapy, ammonia-laden water it went, as soon as I got home. I lifted it out carefully and turned it. It came out clear, bright, and lovely, with not a crack or a chip to mar it.

Over the years dozens of people have exclaimed over my blue and white bowl. I've dipped punch from it at family gatherings and floated water lilies in it plucked from neighborhood ponds by small hands. Fruit has filled it during Thanksgiving dinners, and it has graced many a buffet table at church suppers. Today it sits in a sun-drenched parlor window, the vivid green leaves of a variegate ivy spilling over its sides and along the table.

Like a well-bred woman, my found-treasure adapts to any place or occasion. A lovely piece, it has become an adopted family's heirloom. Keep an eye out. You never know.

A PYGMY MAPLE SYRUP OPERATION

*I remember my youth and the feeling that will
never come back, the feeling that I could last forever,
outlast the sea, the earth and all man.*
—Joseph Conrad,
Youth

A N OUTDOOR FIREPLACE is a lovely thing. Many years ago when my family was busy playing ball, going to band practice and growing, my husband gathered a lot of discarded bricks and built a fireplace in a small grove near the house. It was not a place for barbecuing as today's outside grill is. Rather, it was a place to stoke a fire when the autumn days grew cool, and roast our toes and mellow our spirits as the day came to an end.

There were many evenings we watched the sun go down in a distant field while we poked the embers and told each other stories. Often the kids were off attending some school function, so ol' Dad and I enjoyed the quiet and the chirp of crickets foraging in the nearby garden. Those completely uneventful evenings evoke memories hard to equal.

The hastily contrived fireplace weathered a severe winter, and as the snow dissolved into mire and muck, I watched the winter white melt off its soft, red bricks. I admit to waiting impatiently until we could again take out lawn chairs (and often a wool blanket) for evenings of repose and reflection in the glow of the fire.

Maple syrup time came, and with two large, flourishing trees near the back pasture, we decided to tap for sap for the first time. There was an abundant flow of sap that spring, and before we knew it, far more boiling was needed than we reasoned our kitchen stove could handle.

One morning my husband came home to an early lunch and announced, "I've asked Dod to drop off a pile of slab wood from the sawmill today. I think we can boil some of that sap outdoors—when it's not raining at least—and avoid the kitchen wallpaper peeling off.

"Hooray!" I thought, "We can get out under the sky again—this time the spring sky."

It didn't take long for the neighbor kids to come running when they saw the smoke billowing from behind our small, white home. Many of them had no idea that boiling sap eventually brought maple sugar into existence. They treasured the delicacy on their morning pancakes, but had never given a thought to how the nectar came into being.

It turned out to be a most productive run. Each day for more than three weeks we gathered the tin pails loaded with clear sap. Drip by constant drip would collect something like four gallons of sap a day in each pail. With three spiles in each of the two trees, about 24 gallons a day kept us in the boiling business for quite a time.

Shortly after the kids got in from school we'd walk out back, break some twigs from the dwindling woodpile, and start a fire. Once the flame was healthy we'd uncover the boiling pan, pour the sap accumulation into it and set it a-boil. During the day I'd have worked the boil-down from the past day to where the liquid acquired an amber hue. After a great deal of tasting and letting it cool to estimate the degree of thickening the porridge had acquired, I'd bottle it in small glass containers. You can be certain that, true Yankee that I am, old mayonnaise, pickle and jam jars had been scrubbed and scalded to receive the golden syrup.

After Dad got home from work, and supper was consumed and evening tasks completed, we'd go out to the fireplace. The family would sit on blocks of sawed-off logs and makeshift seats until the evening grew too dark or too cold to continue. Reluctantly we'd take the steaming pan off the fire, cover it with a large aluminum cookie sheet, and leave the dying fire to shrivel and fade in the moisture-laden evening mist.

When the boys had climbed the stairs to bed or school assignments and evening had turned into night, my husband would go back out to the fireplace, carrying the inside boiling pan with him.

Carefully he'd strain the cooled liquor into the pan he carried and bring it back into the house, ready for me to boil down the next morning.

It was definitely a pygmy operation we had going there that spring of 1968, yet it remains a memory of family togetherness , and a time of doing something that was pleasant and resulted in a tangible reward for our labors.

It was a time of sweetness, if you will pardon the pun.

TREASURES
IN SMALL GIFTS

I love the Christmas-tide, and yet,
I notice this, each year I live;
I always like the gifts I get,
But how I love the gifts I give!
　　　　—Carolyn Wells,
　　　　　"A Thought"

 ORTHERN MAINE was slow in recovering from the 1929 stock market crash that created the Depression. In 1935 things were not that much better. Christmas that year looked like a bleak holiday for a mother with two young children. She worked long, hard hours cleaning house for her more affluent friends and neighbors. I have come to believe they could ill afford the pittance they paid her, but it suited them better than giving her charity. My mother was grateful for some way to pay for the small chicken and pork loin she would serve on the feast day.

It is probably a fact of life that we forget the unpleasant and unimportant and remember the things that are good to recall. For the life of me, I have no memory of what was under our small tree that year for me, or what my brother got.

What I do remember is that John and I pooled the small check our errant father sent us each year, and got Mother a fountain pen. She had spoken of her need for one many times. It was an expensive item—it cost something like

$2.50—unbelievable extravagance. We could have held onto our five dollars and treated ourselves many times over, or gone to the Saturday matinee dozens of times. At ten cents a show we felt rich. No, there was genuine excitement in spending our money in a gift that would make Mother happy. Quickly, now; neither of us were such generous kids. We were really quite selfish. We caused Mother no end of anxiety with our bickering and gusty fights, but we were in complete agreement that Mother should have something she would really like.

The small box, hastily wrapped and hidden far at the back of the tree had our undivided attention. We waited until all other bundles were opened before John reached way in back and brought out Mother's gift. The two of us watched with smiling eyes, I suspect, as she slowly pulled away the paper with a statement we had known she would make.

"Oh, you kids should not have spent your money on something for *me!* You have so little yourselves."

All our planning, plotting and secrecy paid off. She was surprised and very obviously delighted with what we had given her. Mother wrote hundreds of letters with that pen. Letters to me while I was away at school, letters to John during his two years serving the U.S. Navy in the Pacific, even a letter or two to my older sons.

The Christmas gift from so long ago still exists. True, it no longer writes: the rubber tube into which you siphoned ink has dried up and cracked; the plunger on the side that activated the ink flow is stuck; the point is bent and would write crooked if it wrote at all.

Somehow I recognized it, among dozens of writing tools I found in Mother's desk as I sorted through them. It is one of those useless items too precious to throw away. One day when a family member paws through *my* accumulations (and I don't envy them the task) they will recognize the uselessness of saving such a tool and chuck it. The memories attached will no longer exist, and it will be sensible to toss it. As long as I remain, however, I suspect the obsolete pen will too.

Some of the best parts of Holiday festivities are the memories we carry away after the tree is down and the mince meat pie is eaten. These memories are almost always of our connections with others.

Think of bringing a small piece of joy to someone who is alone. It doesn't even have to be a gift. A smile or a few words of cheer to a shut-in or a person without family may make a big difference. It amazes me how many there are who truly are alone. They are the ones who need some kind of contact with another human, being no matter how fleeting.

I wish you a life of joy, peace and family connections, with not everything you want. May you have just enough to leave you believing you received "enough" and gave enough, as well, to someone else.

MORE STORIES
PICKED UP
ALONG THE WAY

 ALTHOUGH A RIGHT-LIVING MAN, Roger did not include church attendance among his habits. He did live across the road from the country church and spent many hours grooming the lawns in summer and tending the weekly fires during winter months.

The minister appreciated Roger's good deeds and told him so frequently. One Saturday afternoon as they met in the church, the minister ended their conversation with the question, "Will I see you at the church tomorrow, Roger?"

"You will," was Roger's terse reply.

But alas, there was no Roger present when the minister arrived the next morning. It was not until he carried his sermon text to the pulpit that he saw the scribbled note. It said, "6 A.M. I was here. Where were you?"

 RUTH HAD A SMALL flower/seedling business that was brisk in early spring.

"There were loads of wonderful people who came to buy their spring seedlings," she said. "Only rarely did a real stinker come in, but that was often enough to make a real impression on me."

While telling this brief story Ruth busied herself

pulling weeds from her gigantic flower garden—not an easy task for an 83 year old with a bad knee.

"Well, one day one of these stinkers arrived. A tall, regal lady who wore some kind of cape, so it looked as if she were sailing in. I suspected right off, her nose was too far in the air. We had a delightful calico kitten at that time, and you know, it took an immediate shine to the customer. It twined around a pair of pretty fancy shoes, and was very affectionate.

"I could see the lady was not happy with our kitty. Finally she drew herself up, looked down at the animal, and with steely venom in her voice said, '*I hate cats!*' It was right at that moment that our kitty, looking right at the lady's shoes, threw up all over them.

"My, that was horrid, but somehow it pleased me completely."

CUTS OF MEAT CARRIED different names back when Arthur Boynton sold them in his Water Street, Hallowell market. No one asked for a New York Sirloin, or Top of the Round. The lingo has changed, although such cuts may not be any better than yesterday's.

According to Arthur Boynton, meat was always carefully aged before sale. "We kept a side of beef in the cooler for quite a long time before we sold it. 'Aging' was an important part of getting a good cut of meat.

"I remember Mrs. Marvin calling one day to ask if I would save an English Cut for her. She specified the size and added, 'And I want it well-hung.'"

It was almost a week later that the lady came by for her special cut of meat, properly aged to her demands.

COMMUNITY CHEST volunteers often find their job difficult. One neighbor recounts an unpleasant episode. He rapped at the door of a house on his block and the following "conversation" took place.

"Good morning, Ma'am, I'm collecting for the Community Chest..."

The door banged in his face. He rapped again.

"I'm a volunteer worker for the local Comm..." She slammed the door again.

Now my friend was determined. He rapped a third time. The irate housewife opened the door.

"Madam, I am working—without pay— as a volunteer for your Community Chest. If you insist on insulting me, I expect you to pay me for my time!"

He got a check.

 TWO SCENES THAT BRIGHTENED the holidays: Walking along a dirt road in the hills of Harrison, Maine, we met a middle-aged brother and sister toting a giant Christmas tree on their shoulders. Walking beside them was their father with axe and saw in hand. They had headed into the woods on their rural estate and selected the absolute right tree for the parlor of their brick farmhouse. As they carried the elegant tree along the wooded ridge, a column of twirling gray smoke issued from the center chimney of the house. A wondrous Currier and Ives scene in modern dress.

A brown, shaggy dog clutched a white plastic bag in his teeth as he trotted along Second Street the day after

Christmas. Perhaps there were scents of turkey on paper napkins in the bag. It was obvious the bag was light, filled perhaps with nothing more than discarded gift wrappings. Pooch, however, was intent on carrying the contents home for further investigation. I hope his labors were rewarded, if not by the bag's contents, at least at his family's dinner table!

 WHEN YOU LIVE BESIDE the cemetery you meet a lot of friends on Memorial Day who bring flowers to the graves of their loved ones.

So it was that one year Grace, whose house borders the city burying ground, saw her old friend Mildred placing a bouquet on the grave of her mother-in-law, Jessica. That surprised Grace a little because, as she remembered, Mildred was not especially fond of her husband's mother. Nevertheless, she crossed the street to say hello.

"My, that's a beautiful arrangement, Mildred. Not usual to see such a lovely bunch of white flowers at this time of year."

"They are lovely, aren't they?" answered Mildred. "You're right, white flowers are unusual. I love getting them, though, because Jessica *hated* white flowers!"

 THE CALL HAD GONE OUT that the Governor would be interested in seeing art on a Christmas theme so he might select an appropriate piece for his annual Christmas card.

A talented young artist from Temple submitted two pieces and was pleased to have one of them selected by the chief exec. There was, however, a letter accompanying the notice of selection. The letter said that there would be no pay to the artist for use of the holiday scene, but that the many cards sent would assure great exposure for the artist.

After mulling over the suggestion of no $$$$$ for a week's work and supplies, the young lady responded, "Thank you for your interest in my work. However, as a struggling artist who depends solely on pay for work, I cannot accept your terms. In addition, it is a well known fact that many people *die* of exposure!"

 MAY LEFT HER OFFICE WORK with a small legal firm when her family began arriving. She was completely happy with being a homemaker and didn't give even a passing thought to working outside the home. One day nearly 30 years later, May's former boss called her and asked her to return. There was a vacancy in the staff and they needed someone familiar with the office. May hardly gave it a thought.

Her oldest son was having lunch with her when the call came in. She told Greg about the request as she rejoined him at the table.

"Gorry, Ma, you're not going to even consider such a job, are you? Why, typewriters have changed, probably the bookkeeping system, and I bet you couldn't even take short-hand after all these years. Forget it!" he admonished.

May had considered all these deficiencies on the short walk from the telephone to the kitchen table, and had, until now, had the same thoughts. His comments, however, stopped this valiant lady dead in her tracks. Her reasoning went something like, "He thinks *I can't do it!* Well, little does he know his mother."

They finished their meal, May cleared the table and went back to the phone.

"Hello, Mr. Barrows, this is May. I'll take that job."

She did, and worked, efficiently and effectively, for an additional 15 years.

"MO" IS A BRIGHT, curly headed four year old. Her grandfather owns quarter horses and show Morgans, so the youngster is as comfortable with these creatures as she is with her playmates up the road.

Early in life Mo's family let her lead the horses and almost as soon as she could straddle the smaller ones, she rode. More as a lark than a serious intent, Mo entered a show ring when she was not quite three.

The crowd, as you might expect, loved her. When the ribbons were being awarded, Mo walked up to the judges and, cool as a cucumber, politely accepted a third prize ribbon.

The following year the family let her again show her favorite mount. She took her place beside the horse with the lead in hand. During the lineup she stood at attention and displayed all the characteristics of a true equestrian.

Before the awards are announced each entry parades, in best form, before the judges, pausing long enough for the evaluators to get a good view of the animal.

When Mo's turn came, she did all the right things. She stopped and stood calmly in front of the imposing threesome. As she was about to be passed along, she pointed to the table on which the trophies were displayed, and said with complete candor, "This time, please, I want to get one of those blue ribbons!"

MARGARET PREBLE had been commissioned to do a series of Biblical murals for the Presbyterian Church in Pelham Manor, New York. There were four in all and the last to be completed and perhaps the most extensive was one depicting the Nativity. Following a Sunday morning service shortly after the work was completed, many members of the congregation were waiting to see and comment on the paintings. One very pompous gentleman, rather shy, felt more comfortable speaking to the artist's husband than to the artist herself. Though he intended his conversation to be discreet and private, it was, in fact, conducted in a loud stage whisper.

"Mr. Preble, I certainly do enjoy the work your wife has done here at the church. I am especially fascinated with the Nativity scene. In fact, your wife has the most natural Ass I have ever seen!"

SHORTLY AFTER THIS revealing encounter, a rap came at Margaret's kitchen door one morning. She opened it and found a small boy there.

"Mrs. Preble?"

"Yes, I'm Mrs. Preble. What can I do for you?"

"My name is Joel Banks and I'm eleven years old. I live down the street and I saw the drawing you did of Mrs. Smith. I would like to have you do a drawing of me."

"Why, Joel, I'm very flattered, but are you sure you want to sit still long enough to have a drawing done?"

"Yes, I'm sure, and my father is a doctor and he will operate on you if you'll draw my picture."

"Goodness, that's fine, Joel, but I've had my appendix out and my tonsils and I don't know of anything else that needs to be tended to...."

"Oh, don't worry about that, Mrs. Preble, my father is a very good doctor and he can operate on you fine. He spayed the Heard's cat, and I know he can do just as much for you as any old cat!"

Margaret did indeed draw Joel's picture and knew quite definitely that his mother was unaware of the business transaction. When the drawing was completed, Margaret called Mrs. Banks and invited her in for a cup of coffee. Joel's mother was horrified at her son's boldness. The portrait was given to the family and Margaret felt well repaid by the interesting experience with the eleven year old who was able to come up with such an unusual exchange. To satisfy your curiosity, Dr. Banks never did perform the operation!

 MANY YEARS AGO our home was on the grounds of the Veteran's Administration at Togus. After a sumptuous Sunday dinner I was "walking it off" and passed the greenhouse where patients tended the flowers.

As I passed I greeted a patient who was known for his dedication to growing things. He responded in kind, and went along his way.

Then, bursting with gardening news, he called me back and said, "In August I took a cutting from our only white rose. Since then I've repotted it a couple of times and on the last day of October there was a single white bud on the plant. Today it has two full blossoms and the beginning of two small additional buds. I'm going to take it to the chapel this afternoon just in time for the feast of the Immaculate Conception!"

"That's amazing," I answered. "Do you think that the rose has blossomed so soon because of your green thumb?

The soft-spoken patient shook his head and smiled knowingly. He said nothing, simply winked and pointed his finger heavenward.

IT WAS PERHAPS 1920 or 1925, back when the country store at the crossroads of any Maine town served almost every marketing need. One fall afternoon a customer named Simian came into the store with a downcast look.

"What's the matter, Sim, you look kinda' peaked," Wilt the store owner asked.

"'Tain't me, Wilt, it's Tildy. She's feeling turrible. Thought I'd try to get something to spruce her up a mite. Whatcha' suggest?"

"Well, seeing's how I don't know what ails her, hard to say what to give her, but, say, Sim, Effie just took some ice outa' the ice house and made a batch of ice cream. Now that might perk her up some."

The result was that Sim went home with a small cardboard box filled with ice cream. Effie had gone to some pains to pack the fragile contents in shaved ice so it would stay firm for the two mile carriage ride back to Sim's place.

A few days later Sim came back by the store.

"How's Tildy, Sim?" Wilt asked.

"Some better."

"How'd she like the ice cream you took her?"

"Well, sir, that was right cold. She didn't like it a bit at first, but I took it into the kitchen and het it up almost to boiling and it suited her to a 'T.'"